T0103534

Intimidating Obscurity

Intimidating Obscurity

A Pursue to Eternity

DIMPLE SINGH

PARTRIDGE

ISBN:	Softcover	978-1-4828-8760-0
	eBook	978-1-4828-8759-4

Print information available on the last page.

To order additional copies of this book, contact
Partridge India
000 800 10062 62
orders.india@partridgepublishing.com

www.partridgepublishing.com/india

In the still and sinister hours of darkness,
We walked and walked without uttering a word,
He held my hand and I stared him all this while
We paused and sat under the shade of a tree.

An hour passed by and we had no conversation,
Taking the first step I whispered "I Love You"
He was disturbed yet astonished,
He kissed my cheeks and said, "I Love You Too."

That was the last moment I spoke,
The last moment I saw the world with my eyes,
He left me the next moment forever,
And my lifeless soul refused to live
until he returns again.

Acknowledgement

This is the first book that I wrote and it would have been impossible to complete this book without the accompaniment and guidance of a few people. They had helped me at each and every step and given me the will power and determination to write this book.

I offer my first vote of thanks to my parents. My mother, Kalpana Singh, and my father, Vijay Singh, have been an endless support and the strength of my life. Their love encouraged me to overcome all the hurdles of my life with zeal. My maternal uncle Dr. Shailendra Singh has also been a constant support throughout my life. It was he who always had faith in me and made me realize my strengths and weaknesses.

Lastly I would like to offer a huge vote of thanks to all my friends- Akanksha Singh, Musba Hashmi, Soheib Ahsan, Kiran Vallabh, Srijita Chakrabarty, Vani Gulati, Saumya Surbhi, Nilabh Mozumdar, Kartikey Kashyap, Prerna Singh, Jasleen Joseph, Tanya Trehan, Aliza Zafar, Snehal Zare, Priya Anwesha and Nabhneel Tiwary for their constant support.

Preface

'Intimidating Obscurity: A Pursue to Eternity' is a short novella highlighting the theme of selfless love and sacrifice. Every ambitious woman feels that a guy's presence is can ruin her career. So was the belief of Stella Stewart. She never expected to fall in love with anyone. The day she fell in love with Rey she bestowed her life to him only to get betrayal in return.

I, Dimple Singh, believe in true love. My heart was broken deeply. I too fell in love with someone who left me to weep forever without even bothering to look back even once. He knew that it was only he who could get me out of that state. Yet he refused to enter my life again. He might have broken my heart but he failed to break me entirely. I woke up and one day and realized that there's lots ahead waiting for me to bloom and bloom.

I decided to make my biggest weakness my strength. At that very moment I held my lucky pen in my hand and initiated to write this novel. I gave this book the title of 'Intimidating Obscurity A Pursue to Eternity' coz in this book Stella Stewart ends up losing her life in order to pursue the true love of her lover. Despite her death her love remained eternal.

The person who broke my trust gave me the reason to smile again. All the gates of love are still open in my heart and I still believe that there is someone who will heal all the wounds caused by an artificial love by showering the sprinkles of true love on me.

I don't abhor the person. Today I would like to thank him coz it was his absence that became my strength and motivated me to write this novella.

Chapter I

"Stella, are you alright? I hope you'll understand that Rey is my love, my first love. So if you'll ever try to cross my way you'll have it from me and from my husband, Rey. Wish you a very blissful married life," warned Kimaya.

"Don't fret Kimaya. I'm not doted towards your husband."

Most probably that was the very last time I met her. I saw her figure thriving as she walked away from me. It was quarter to six. Robert must be waiting for me. It was too late. I was married to him today morning. I hurried homewards.

For a woman the marriage is considered as the best phase of her life. Every woman waits eagerly for the day when she hands over her entire life to the man she loves. The embraces of our lover gives us the feeling us the pleasure that one tries to find in heaven. The same was not the case with me. My story is entirely different. I married the man whom I hate the most. He was the villain of my life. His wicked devil smile and his foul breath and words can kill any human being in the fraction of a second.

No sooner did I open the door of my house than he grabbed my hand. He pulled me closer and clinched me. His fingers stroked the curls of my hair and down they reached my lips. I closed my eyes. He was urging for a kiss but I refused immediately.

"Don't cross the line. You know it better that why we're married and under what circumstances I was forced to marry a demon like you. So stay miles away from me. It will be the best remedy for your evil sickness. I'm leaving right now."

No sooner did I turn the other side than he grasped my arm. He lifted his hands and slid them over my waist.

"You can't do this to me. This is not happening, alright. Either you buzz off right now or let me go. Stop taking advantage of my helplessness."

I switched off the lights immediately and requested him to sleep. This night was one of the worst nightmares of my life. You must be wandering that why I'm doing this? I'm married to Robert. Then what was the reason that I had to do all this, especially when I know that I love someone else? If ever I get a blessing of a wish I would desire only and only his death. I wish I could step out of this slaughter house forever. Though I'm alive yet my presence in this house kills me each and every second.

It all started three years ago when I was an independent and gay woman.

"Stella you've done a fabulous job, you are simply amazing. You are intellectual at all things. I still can't believe that you've solved this conundrum just in a go. Even the most brilliant teachers of this institute have failed to do so," complimented Miss Briganza.

Miss Briganza is one of my favourite educators in this schooling institute. She has always been different from others, it may be in teaching or guiding her students or understanding her students. She has always been considerate and supportive towards her students. She has never supported the corruption and treachery of other teachers. She is just the best. She is more than a friend to me than a teacher. She has maintained her exquisite personality and traits, which is impossible to maintain at an age of 44. This was my last day of schooling. The board results were to be announced today and my heart beat was increasing rapidly as the time of announcement came nearer. After a few minutes I saw my principal stepping forward with a sheet in his hands. She held our results in her hands.

She announced", Stella Stewart, rank #1, 99.7%. She has topped at the national level. Congratulations Stella. We all are proud of you. Please come forward and collect your reward."

I was flushed with intense delight. I rushed towards her. She hugged me and gave me an offering. She wished me luck and safe journey. After an hour almost all the results were announced. Some students shouted with glee while the rest weeped with sorrow. I was bewildered whether to sympathize with those who were sobbing or to celebrate with those who are mesmerizing. At last I decided to party and celebrate this last day of 12th standard. I was wandering how mom would react after knowing my result. She will surely hug me proudly.

My mom was my only family. My father died in a car accident when I was just six months old. It was my mom who brought me up all alone and also managed to be one of the most successful businesswomen of the country.

I would not tell her now about my score. I want to surprise her with my result. I want her to be present in front of me when I would be informing her about my result. For the timing I went to Serena, my childhood companion.

"Congrats Stella, you've surpassed. So what are your plans for your future."

"I have to do medical for my mom. I've assured her that I'll do what she'll ask me to."

"Why do you sound as if you are not convinced with the medical course?"

"I am actually not convinced. Though I've scored well, yet I feel I am forcing myself. My passion is acting, music, dance, fame, etc and not medical."

"Then why are you doing this?"

"I told you, for my mom's sake. My mom is my family. She has devoted her entire life to me and so it's my duty to fulfill her dream."

"Why?"

"Let's cut it out. I don't want to discuss this any further. I'm leaving. Goodbye."

"Hey, Stella there's still time. Come on it's our last day."

"No Serena it's already too late and I have to travel back to Chicago. It's almost time for my flight."

"Take care, I'll miss you friend."

"I'll miss you too. Hope to meet you soon in future."

"Bye."

"Bye."

So that was the end of my last schooling day. I was mature enough now. How would the college life be? Though it seems to be interesting yet I can't be predictable. It was eight now. I was seated inside my flight. I was completely disoriented in the thoughts of the new twist in life that was waiting for me ahead. I was about to sleep when I was disturbed by a call in my cell.

"Hello, Stella Stewart this side. Who are you?"

"I'm sorry to inform you that your mom has passed away an hour ago."

"What?"

"Yes, your mom, Julie Stewart, is dead."

"How?"

"Reach here as soon as possible. I'll let you know everything soon."

At once my eyes were overflowing with moan. The day that was full of joy, ended with complete mourning. Till now I was only living for my mom. She was the only one I loved the most in this world. She was my only savior. I wish I could at least meet her for the last time. Everything seemed to lose life now. I was almost pale now. What went wrong all of a sudden? Is it a natural death, a suicide, or a MURDER. My thoughts were totally baffled right now. I could feel nothing at all. All I knew is that I've lost my mom forever and she'll never come back again. I have to face the realism. I have to be firm. My mom would never desire me to go pale like this. At once I consoled myself. After a few hours I reached Chicago. As soon as I got down I rushed where my mom was lying dead. I saw many people crowded near her and cops waiting for me. My friend Suzena hugged me and cried aloud.

"I'm sorry for you Stella."

"Don't be. All I want to know is how she died."

One of the policemen stepped forward.

"She was murdered."

"Who killed her? I'll kill that bastard."

"We are still searching for him. We'll try our best."

"How do you know she was murdered?"

"There are scars found on her neck. It seems as if someone tried to choke her to death."

"Find that person as soon as possible. I swear I won't spear that person."

"Leave that on us."

"According to Miss Julie's statement on these documents her property is yours now."

"What will I do with this property when mom's not here anymore? This house will be incomplete without her."

"That's up to you."

"I don't want it."

"You don't have a choice."

"Alright."

"We'll be waiting at your residence. We need your signatures on certain documents at home."

"Sure. I'll be there soon."

Suzena tried to soothe me up but all in vain. I was caught in the arms of intense gloominess which I found unfeasible to break out from. I walked beside a road where I called for a taxi. I got inside. The driver asked me where to go. For a moment there was complete silence inside. Then I told him the location of my residence and he took me there. As soon as I reached my residence I began to observe it. It was magnanimous. It was avast, silver and gold in shade. I went inside. The furniture was well-furnished and all the equipments were branded. But what would I do of this residence when there is no one to stay with me? I don't need anything. All I want is my mom back. After a few minutes the cops stepped in and one of them bought forward a few documents.

"Miss Stella Stewart this vast property is now yours. Please sign on these documents."

"Congratulations Stella you are an absolute proprioter now."

"If you are done with all this could you please leave me alone?"

"Sure."

"Remember to inform me about the executioner as soon as you catch hold of him or her."

"We surely will. Take care. If you suspect anyone do inform us too?"

"Yeah."

"If you want we can make arrangements of security over here?"

"There's no need for it. Thanks."

Chapter 2

"I love you James."

"I love you too Serena."

"It's been six years since we've been dating each other. I trust you. I love you. So today I propose you. Will you marry me James?"

"Not so soon baby."

"Why? Are you committed to someone else?"

"Are you nuts?"

"Then what's the matter baby?"

"I don't think it's the right time."

"Why?"

"Serena it's too early to get married. I think we should wait for a few more years. We are not mature enough to handle situations presently so how will we handle such a big responsibility of marriage? Please understand, don't take me wrong. I love you a lot but at this point of time I don't wish to get married."

"Maybe you are right."

"Hey, don't be upset. I'll marry you one day and I promise it will be the best marriage ever of our life."

"Alright baby I trust you."

"So what are your plans for today?"

"No plans for today."

"So let's make it great. I'll take you out on a dinner date today. What say?"

"Well, I don't wish to go on a date with you today."

"Why?"

"Don't you think it's too soon."

"So now you are tormenting at me."

"No."

"Then what?"

"First you propose me in a decent way then I'll agree."

"What hogwash is it? I'm not doing this. You got to be kidding right."

"Then go on a date with someone else."

"Come on."

"Fine then I'll be dating someone else."

"I accept myself as defeated."

"You can never defeat me."

"Listen will you be my date tonight."

"You can do better than this."

"Serena, will you be my date tonight?"

"Are you commanding me?"

"Serena, please will you be my date tonight?"

"Yes sweetheart."

"Thankfully you agreed. You women are almost impossible and so unpredictable to be easily understood."

"You guys are….."

"Shut up."

"Really, do you want me to go?"

"No."

"Gotcha."

Their sweet and romantic conversation was interrupted by the doorbell. Somebody was outside.

"Honey I'll be back soon."

Serena went downstairs and rushed to open the door. She saw police force gathered before her house.

"Are you Miss Serena?"

"Yes."

"I hope you know who is Stella?"

"Of course, she's my very close companion. Why? What's the matter inspector?"

"Her mom is dead. She has been murdered."

"Oh my God!"

"If you don't mind please may I inquire something related to Stella and her mother?"

"Sure."

She showed them the way to her living room and requested them to take a seat. She saw James walking down the stairs. She was aware of what he actually felt that moment. She knew it that he was full of rage as his romance was been interrupted. She went forward to James and whispered softly in his ears.

"James they are the investing officers of Stella's mom's murder case. They want to inquire about Stella."

"That's not done Serena. You've ruined all my plans."

"It's just a matter of a few minutes."

"Bunk it."

"Wait."

"I'm leaving now but I'll be waiting for you tonight. I hope you won't disappoint me this time."

"You're overreacting. It's nothing to meddle about. My bestie needs me and all I know is that I have to be with her today."

"So are you leaving?"

"No way James I love you."

The policeman yelled at Serena, "Ma'am we have lots of other things to do and numerous cases to solve. There are yet many more cases we have to solve and investigate on. So will you mind hurrying?"

"James I'll be right back. Don't leave."

Serena went up to them.

"Miss Serena, tell us everything you know about Stella."

"There are lots of things. At this point of time I don't know where to start from."

"Tell us something about her personal life."

"Why are you asking me about her personal life? Why don't you ask her instead?"

"Was she ever disturbed?"

"Nope. There is not even a single cause that has ever seemed to distract her. She has no boyfriend. She does not regret the fact that she is single. She has always been living alone and gleefully."

"Serena tell us something more. If her mother has been murdered then I'm scared that even her life is at a risk right now."

"What?"

"Yeah that's true. She's already terrified by all that had happened to Mrs. Julie. This is the reason why we are here to enquire about her life."

"I'll incontestably help you."

"Please tell us more."

"Stella has always been a studious and talented person undoubtedly. She has never been disturbed by anything. She wanted to fulfill her mom's desires and expectations and she did it. I'm so sorry for her. I don't think so she was engaged in anything else. She has no enemy nor does she have hard feelings for anyone. She is pure-hearted."

"Thank you so much for your co-operation."

"Anytime sir."

"Take care ma'am."

As soon as they left she walked upstairs and called for James. But he had already left. She gave a call to him by her cell phone. He did not receive her calls. She even texted him. He did not reply. That night she did not sleep. The whole night she wondered over James's suddenly changing attitude towards her.

Before the sunrise she murmured a few words and reached for her cell phone. Though she was aware that James was asleep at that moment, yet she could not restrain herself from making another attempt. Maybe even James had not slept the whole night. She rang him up with every ringing sound her heartbeat increased. She was right. This time James did receive her call.

"James I'm sorry."

"No baby, I'm sorry. Let's go out for lunch today."

"Only on one condition."

"Do I have to propose you again?"

"No....no....I'll tell you my condition once you are before my sight."

"I'll be right there very soon."

"Come soon. You know very well that I'm an impatient woman."

"Of course I know that."

"I was not able to sleep last night."

"That's my fault, after all you only dream about me every night."

"Very funny."

"I can understand. I am sorry."

"Don't waste your time only apologizing. I won't forgive you if you are late today. Hurry up. You have only one hour to reach at my place and pick me up. Your time starts now."

"Sure.....byeeee."

"Bye."

Chapter 3

After three days of complete depression I convinced myself. My life has not ended yet. One has to move on in life. I can't be frail. I'll make sure that the culprit is behind the bars soon.

I finally decided to join the college. I won't do medical. Though it was my mom's last desire yet I was aware that medical is not my cup of tea. So I would only opt for music. The musical notes were waiting in joyful anticipation to be sung by me, those instruments to be played by me and success to be withheld in my fist forever.

I entered the gates of the college, passed through the corridor and entered the hall to attend the first college lecture of my life. The professor was late. I was looking around to find a place for myself. To my surprise I found Kimaya, my one of the closest childhood friend. When I went near her she looked at me with a daze.

"Stella," she shouted, "What a pleasant surprise?"

"I'm pleased to meet you too."

"This time it has really been a long duration."

"Seriously."

"Where have you been all these years? How is your mom?"

"She has passed away."

"I'm sorry."

"Don't be."

"But how?"

"She was murdered."

"By whom?"

"The investigation is still going on and I swear I'm going to eat his heart once I find him."

"I too won't spear him."

"I'm all alone nowadays."

"You are no more alone now."

"Thanks."

"Anytime."

"Tell something about your life also."

"Nothing great. Just the same boring routine."

After a long conversation our professor finally arrived. We all sat down silently. Our professor appeared to be rigorous.

"Good morning everyone."

No body replied. The sight amused me.

"Shameless. None of you know how to respect your teachers. But things will change now because I believe in sterness."

I whispered into Kimaya's ears, "he is so bugging."

"Seriously."

He pointed at us and yelled, "Get up and get out of my class both of you."

"We are sorry, sir."

"It's too late to apologise. Don't argue further and leave."

Both of us stepped out of the classroom at once. Though he appeared to be stern yet it was fun to be punished on the first day of college. We both stood outside and giggled. After a few minutes he himself called us back and we uttered sorry and went to our seats.

"Not that one. You both seem to be mischievous. You both won't sit together."

We replied, "Okay."

Mr. Gill ordered me to sit next to a guy. After being seated I had a short glance over him. He was quite fair, with a dashing appearance, his eyes were glistening and so dazzling that once lost in the depth can never hope to be back again. He had an outstanding physique. When he felt that I am staring him he gave me a stern look. I immediately turned my face in the opposite direction. I heard the professor calling me out.

"Stella where the hell, are you lost again? If you don't want to study then get out right now."

"Sir I promise you that this won't be repeated."

"I hope not."

"Sorry."

"Last chance Stella."

After attending his boring lecture I was about to go to Kimaya. Rey stopped me.

He said, "Why were you staring me during the lecture. I hate it when girls stare me. Were you checking me out?"

With a stern look I replied, "Excuse me, I'm not interested in you. It was just……"

"I was just kidding."

I told myself thank God or else he would have thought that I'm checking him out.

"Stella, are you with me?"

"I'm sorry."

"No issue, I noticed you several times. You are seriously a lost case."

"I'm not."

My conversation with him was disturbed by Kimaya.

Kimaya said, "Stella let's go or are you planning to stay here the entire day?"

"Of course, not."

"Hi Rey."

"Hey Kimaya."

"Do you both know each other?"

Kimaya replied, "Yes I do know him. We first met in a pub where I was completely inebriated. He was the one who dropped me home that night since I was not able to drive. Next day I invited him for dinner and this is how our friendship grew."

"That's great."

"Rey, why don't you join us for dinner tonight?"

"Again."

"Why not?"

"Okay, I'll be there tonight. What time?"

"Nine."

"Alright. See you tonight then."

"Bye."

After he left I murmured to Kimaya, "Why did you call him for dinner tonight?"

"So what?"

"I'm not ready to dine with a stranger."

"Oh common, he's your friend too."

"He's not my friend."

"Whatever?"

"If he'll come then I won't"

"Stella you are overreacting. It's good to socialize with people around you. Learn to trust people."

"Fine, I'll be there but only because you are inviting me. He is really weird. He thinks I like him. How can such a weird person be your friend? It's surprising."

"Hahaahah. He's fun to be around. He's a sweetheart."

"A SWEETHEART. It is the funniest thing I've ever heard. I don't find him interesting at all."

"I bet you that you'll change your point of view about him once you become his friend and this will happen tonight. I'll make sure you both become friends. See you tonight then."

After sometime I reached home. There I found Serena crying hysterically. She came forward and hugged.

"What's the matter Serena?"

"Sorry to hear about your loss."

"Don't be sorry. I'm glad to see you."

"How are you?"

"I'm better now."

"Stella I need to leave. I just came to meet you after hearing about your present condition."

"Please stay. We'll have fun."

"Some other day. Actually I have some other plans for today."

"Are you dating someone?"

"We are already in a relationship."

"Well, that's a great news. Why didn't you tell me before? Anyways who's the lucky one?"

"It's James."

"I don't know him but promise me that next time you'll introduce me to him."

"Definitely. Take care bye."

Before I could utter a word more she left hurridly. I can understand why she reacted like that. This is what happens when one is in love. I looked at the clock. It struck half past seven. I was late. I need to dress up for dinner at Kimaya's place. But what to wear? This is what irritates me the most –dressing up for parties, celebrations and at times even casual dinner. It took me an hour to dress up. After an hour I reached Kimaya's residence.

She greeted me warmly. Rey was already present. I was extremely late.

Kimaya hugged me and whispered in my ears, "I thought you won't come."

I replied, "I had to, after all my bestie had invited me."

"Hi Rey."

"Hi Stella."

This time I could not get my eyes off Rey. He looked out of this world. The words were too scanty to describe him this time. He even noticed me staring at him weirdly. I tried to control my eyes not to stare at him but they have already beated my brain. Rey felt a bit unnerving this time and even I realized that what I was doing was peculiar. It would give him wrong signals. So I finally faced the opposite direction. After a few seconds I rolled my eyes in his direction. To my surprise this time he was gazing at me. Slowly and slowly I again faced him. He was indulged too. We had an eye to eye contact for a few minutes, lost in a different world. I would have loved to admire him further when Kimaya called us outside. The dinner was ready.

As I was leaving he whispered in my ears, "You are quite adorable." I gave him a huge lusty smile.

"Let's go."

"Sure, ladies first."

"I like it."

"And I like you."

"Excuse me."

"I mean I like your voice. It's soothing, charming and of course appealing."

"Thanks."

We sat at the dining table I was seated opposite to him but facing him. Kimya sat next to him. We had endless conversations while eating and after the dinner was over Rey pleaded to leave as it was too late. I was about to leave too but Kimaya stopped me. After Rey had left, she grabbed my right hand and led me to a room.

"Kimaya I think that it's too late. I should leave. I'll talk to you tomorrow."

"Stay over here for today."

"Why?"

"Just like that. Can't I spend some time with you?"

"You can. Alright, I'll stay."

"What do you want to discuss about?"

"He's someone special."

"Really, please tell his name."

"I'm feeling shy."

"Tell. I'm eager to know that person's name whose ruling your heart."

"There is correct time for everything. I'll tell you very soon but not now. Presently I need your help."

"I'll only help you if you'll tell me the name."

"That guy is Rey."

"Rey."

"I love him."

"When did this happen?"

"He's so vehement."

"But Kimaya I think he's not of your type."

"Why?"

"You deserve someone better."

"I don't think so. Rey is the best match for me. I want to be his girlfriend."

"Don't be stupid."

"You're so callus. I am asking you for a help and instead of helping me you ..."

"Fine I'll help you."

She gave me a hug and shouted gleefully. The entire night our conversation was only of Rey. I was not able to comprehend why I was feeling so invidious. I was a bit disturbed for some time. The day we envy our best friend only for a guy then it's a crystal clear indication that we are in love with that guy. This is the reason why we are not able to see that person being loved and given importance by someone else.

I hope I'm not in love with him. I told myself Stella control your sentiments. Rey is not of my type either. I should maintain a distance with him. Kimaya is my best friend. I must get both of them closer. Why am I thinking about all this? I don't love him though I like him a bit. It won't make a difference.

Chapter 4

"Hey Stella."

"Hey Serena."

"Tell me more about your life."

"It's perfect now. I've decided to go for auditions today."

"Which auditions?"

"I always wanted to be a popstar, a rockstar and of course a superstar. Today is the chance, the first and last chance."

"Wish you all the very best."

"Thank you."

"I wish that…."

Suddenly she yelled while I was talking to her through my cell. When I shouted out her name she didn't reply. After a few seconds the call was disconnected. When I tried to contact her again the number did not existed. I was aware that something was erroneous. I dashed towards my vehicle and instructed the driver to rush to Serena's dwelling. I must reach there as soon as possible and before something terrible happens. Astonishingly when I reached there I saw her cadaver lying on the ground. I was completely petrified after this unpleasant incident. First my mom passed away and now even Serena was dead. I dashed towards her dead corpse and shed tears. I informed the cops about the incident and within a few minutes they too arrived at the site.

One of them inquired, "You are Stella, right?"

"Yes Sir."

"Ah, the very same person whose mom had expired infact eradicated to death a few days ago."

"Yes."

"Now even Serena died."

"Yes."

"I fail to understand that why are you interlinked with all the murders?"

"What are you trying to say?"

"We are not suspecting you. We are really sorry for your loss again. We are just trying to help you out by getting this case solved. I think you should leave for now. Let us handle the whole situation."

I know that it is not the appropriate time to think about the auditions but I have to leave right now. Ignoring everything, I reached the studio and successfully got selected. I signed the contract. Now I was a vocalist. From tomorrow onwards I have to perform on the stage before the whole audience. Serena's death was unexpected and hear-rendering. But I can't lose my potency. That night seemed to be so depressive. I had a platform and my talent was about to be recognized by people. Yet my life seemed to be so incomplete. The two deaths were lurid and frightful. I wandered whether both the murders were committed by the same person.

Next morning I woke up early I even invited Rey and Kimaya to attend my first show positively. There, I met my instructor.

He explained, "This is your first show Stella. All the best and don't mess it up anyhow."

I replied, "Don't worry you won't be disheartened."

He said, "I trust you. Ten minutes more."

He left after instructing me and biding me luck. I was a bit nervous. I peeped through a small opening of the curtains that were leaning on the stage. I noticed Kimaya seated in joyful anticipation. Rey was not present. I was dejected. I heard the host of this event proceeding with the show. It was time. After five minutes the curtains drew open. The whole spectators glanced at me. Their eyes were completely fixed on me. With a deep sigh I began confidently. In the middle of my performance I saw Rey before my sight. My confidence grew.

After my performance everyone applauded and appreciated my voice. When I went backstage I was congratulated for my success. Even Kimaya and Rey congratulated me. I decided to treat both of them for my first hit and invited them to my house around eight that night. They agreed.

As soon as I reached home I instructed all the servants to handle all the preparations. Around six thirty, I received a call from Kimaya informing me that she won't be able to attend my dinner party tonight. This meant that only I and Rey will be present tonight, all alone. I tried to explain my heart this is not correct. He is Kimaya's soulmate, although neither of them has proposed each other till now. Control yourself Stella.

The door bell rang. I went downstairs to open the door. Rey although appeared dashing regularly but today he looked extraordinary. He has never looked so attractive before. He was wearing a cut sleeves jet black colored leather jacket covering a trendy designer shirt within and navy blue jeans.

"Rey please come inside."

We both sat still for a few minutes. The awkward silence disturbed me so I began the conversation.

"Rey Kimaya…."

"I know she won't be here."

"Shall I get you a drink?"

"A small one."

As I was heading towards the kitchen he requested me to stay and sit. I sat down on the couch. I insisted on knowing the reason. He didn't reply. Some thought seemed to disturb him.

He hesitatingly said, "You look stunning today."

"Thanks. Is that all?"

"No."

"I think I should get a drink and then you can tell me whatever you want to."

"Please stay, I need to talk to you about this right now."

"Speak up."

He stood and came forward to me. He then sat next to me and held my hand. He pulled me closer and kissed my hand.

"Stella Stewart I love you."

I didn't believe what I heard. It was true, all true. He loved me and I loved him. I accept that I love him too. That moment was so alluring. These three words made my day.

I replied with a smile, "I love you too Rey."

"I've been in love with you since the first time I met you. It was not you who stared me. It was me who could not get my eyes off you. I admit it that I still can't get my eyes off you."

He lifted his hand and placed his fingers on my lips. Then slowly he touched and felt it. Without thinking much I bent forward and kissed him. For a few minutes I forgot that he was my best friend's first love and I was lost in the passionate kiss that our lips shared and felt. I never wanted things to pause but guilt appeared in my mind and I had to stop suddenly. I realized that I was cheating Kimaya. I promised her make Rey fall in love with her and I myself was striking at him. I pushed him backwards.

"What's the matter Stella?"

"I'm sorry Rey but I can't cheat Kimaya. I never told you but I think it will better is I tell you everything honestly. Kimaya loves you too maybe more than me and I believe that you deserve her love and not mine."

"Stella I like her but as a friend. She's just my friend and I cannot imagine her beyond that in my life. I love you only. So don't sacrifice your love for anyone's sake. Love is selfish."

"But I can't."

Before I can utter a word more he gave me a soft kiss on my cheeks and I paused.

"I'm sure Kimaya will understand and would join us in our happiness too."

"I hope so."

"Stella today we are all alone. So let's have some fun."

"No way."

We were about to kiss again when my phone started to ring. I received the call. Why did I receive the call? I did not know that the call would alter my life forever. I stood almost dead and after placing the receiver back to its position I headed towards the living room as slowly as possible. Rey was waiting for me eagerly.

"Stella who was it?"

"Rey it's too late. You should leave."

"Stella but…"

"Just leave."

"Before that I wanted to ask you will you marry me?"

"Leave right now. I'll reply tomorrow."

"If you want me to leave I'll do as you say but I want your answer tomorrow morning. Tomorrow I'll confess before the entire college that we love each other."

"We'll talk tomorrow."

"Goodnight."

He leaned forward and gave me a goodnight kiss. I didn't stop him this time because I was aware that this was our last kiss and maybe the last moment when we both are together. As his figure disappeared I shed my tears and lay on my bed. I felt so helpless at that moment. I wish I could have stopped him. All I could say was "GOODBYE REY."

Chapter 5

Kimaya was mesmerized in Rey's love or one could probably say that she was madly in yearn of him. The thoughts of having him in her life was the most pleasing thought and all she wanted was that her dreams get hold of reality soon. That night she was feeling restless. She kept on rolling from one side of the bed to another. She could not glimpse anything except for the pipe dreams in which only Kimaya and Rey existed. She only desired to - hear his voice, become disoriented in his dreams, sense the soothing touch when he lays his hand over hers. Her thirst for his charm and the want to heed those three magical words from his orifice made her an impatient soul. She was so disturbed that night that she could not think about anything except for the moments that she had spent with him.

"That's it", she told herself. "Tomorrow would be the day that I was awaiting for since so long. I will propose the love of my life tomorrow morning before the entire college. He will definitely accept my love after all I am rich, stunning and sharp and I have all the qualities within me that a man always seeks for in his girlfriend. I must sleep now."

With a big smirk on her face she shut her eyelids and slept peacefully.

On one side Kimaya was building her castles in air, on the other side I was feeling dejected. I designed out the best way to get rid of Rey's proposal before the entire university tomorrow morning. In case he intends to do as he had mentioned before leaving I will reject him and scorn at him until he finally hates me. Alas! This was the end of all. We are not meant to be together. I was my own enemy who was creating a total mess of her life. I am caught in the devil's trap.

The next day I rose up early and tried to delay everything as much as possible as I was not sure how to deal with Rey today. I just want to maintain a huge distance with him not by choice but by the irony of my life. I was about to enter my college building when someone laid his hands above my eyes and covered them fully. I struggled to set myself free. After a minute he removed his hands. He was Rey.

He whispered in my ears, "You kept me waiting for a quite a long time today. No more waiting now coz in a minute every human being inside this campus will shower their good wishes for our new love."

I was astonished. I pulled his hand firmly and said, "Don't do that."

"Don't be shy. I have made all the arrangements."

"If you'll do so you'll lose me forever."

"Why are you being so shy Stella? Common, don't stop me. Stop yourself instead who's interrupting my thoughts and actions again and again. I can never lose you lady coz you're mine forever and this the entire world will know."

"Why don't you understand?"

"Understand what?"

"You and I are just not meant to be together."

With an alarming look on his face he questioned, "Why? Who told you so? Stella Stewart I love you more than myself, more than any reason, more than anything else in the world. I will die if you'll leave me."

"C'mon nobody dies coz of a simple rejection. You can't compel me to love you or be in a relationship with you. If you'll not stop right now trust me you'll regret this moment for the rest of your life and I'm genuinely serious about this."

"Stop kidding right now and be serious."

"I am serious Rey. I don't love you. Can't you get it at once? Why are you forcing me to do what I don't want to?"

"No you are lying to me."

"I'm not."

"If you are not lying then tell me that what was all that? What about our kiss? What was all that? I saw the love for me in your eyes last night."

"Stop acting like an immature person. I was drunk last night so I might have said all that. I am not at all interested in all this. I just consider you as a friend that's it. Don't expect anything beyond this from my side at least."

"So all that has happened yesterday was just an act of pretence for you?"

"Of course it is. I don't have time for all this bullshit."

"If all this seems like a waste to you then answer me honestly that why don't you love?"

"Again you've started all this nonsense. If you insist so much let me notify you that I already love someone else."

"Who's the lucky one?"

"I don't consider it important to answer you all that."

He grabbed both my arms firmly and it was hurting me pathetically. I screamed, "Rey you're hurting me."

"Now you understand that how much hurt I am. This is the amount of pain that a broken heart has to go through after every second of rejection."

"I never committed that I love you. Stop torturing me now you moron."

While we were still on with our quarrel I saw people staring us. All were gathered. Seeking the opportunity I managed to push him away.

One of them asked, "What's going on Rey?"

Rahul yelled, "Rey you ordered me to collect everyone in the campus and now ..."

Arushi said, "You wanted to tell the entire college something special. What is it?"

I saw Kimaya struggling through the crowd to comprehend and insisted on knowing the matter. At once I mapped a plan. I went to Kimaya and urged her to follow me. She did as I said.

Kimaya asked. "Please can somebody tell me what's going on?"

I replied, "Kimaya I had a conversation with Rey last night about you and I'm glad to say that he agreed. He wanted to admit in front of all of us that how much he loves you." I turned my face towards him and added, "I hope I'm right Rey. How will you answer? Kimaya he's kind of diffident."

Kimaya hugged me and whispered, "You are really a true bestie and thanks for everything. You are a cupid. But how did you manage to convince him for all this?"

"Ask the person with whom you have to spend the rest of your life. He will narrate you everything in detail."

While I hugged her, I faced Rey and I could notice clearly in his eyes that he was broken deeply. It seemed as if his eyes wanted to convey to me that he loves me so much and wanted me to accept his love. I too wanted to apologize to him and accept his proposal with an intense kiss but nothing can be changed now. Kimaya went up to Rey and was persisting for a kiss. But he stepped backwards.

He said, "I need some time so that I could know you well."

"You're so endearing. I don't mind. Take as much time as you want after all you are all mine."

"Stella." He faced me and passed out a sarcasm, "Thanks for everything. You were right. I will never forget this for the rest of my life."

"He's right Stella thank you."

Everyone left except for me. I fell on my knees and wept over my misfortune. I want to stop him. My heart yelled "Please don't leave me. I love you more than my life. I love you so much that I can even leave you. And I can never fall in love with anyone else but only you. I'll love you till my heart stops beating. Maybe we are not together but my love for you will never fade and it's a promise. Goodbye Rey but only for now."

I was not comfortable attending the lectures that day so I left early. When I entered my house I was scandalized. The living room was totally messed up. As I was walking the main door slammed behind me with a bang. I was terrified and immediately turned back. I expected someone to be there but I saw nobody. It amazed me. I was unaware of all that was happening that day.

I felt that someone was keeping an eye on me 24*7. I wandered that someone is definitely after my life now. First he killed my mom, then my dearest friend Serena. He's always killed those who've been close to my heart. I just hope that his next target is not Rey. I don't fear anyone. I love him and nobody in this world can dare to even touch him in my presence. That culprit must take my life first before he can harm him anyhow. Before he executes out some other plan I must think of something to get rid of all nuisance.

I entered the bedroom. Everything was perfect out there but it made me ponder over the issue that why didn't he ruin my bedroom. I was extremely disturbed at that point of time. So I decided to bathe. Maybe it might refresh me. I have to be fragile and must act like one else it will become arduous for me to deal with all this. Once I'll gain victory over all this then I'll convey to Rey about all that had happened and finally I'll utter before him those three magical words.

This positive emotion of winning his love back flushed within me a sense of self assertion. The shower was open and the water droplets refreshed my mind. While I was bathing I felt someone peeping in. But whenever I turned back I noticed no one. Maybe it's just my self -consciousness that is painting out such a faint picture in front of my sight. Why am I so nervous? Miss Stella Stewart does not fear anyone. Who can enter my residence without my permission? Even if somebody does I will screw his life. I held the towel in my hands and wiped my body gently. I again sensed someone peeping in but I ignored this time.

I went to the bedroom and sat in front of the mirror. I was reminded of the time when I used to be beauty cautious every now and then but now I am so ashamed of myself that I can't even have a look at myself in the mirror. I quickly ended up what was required and sat calmly on my couch. I remained silent for some time, sitting still and thought that I have to save him. He's the next victim of all these cases. His life is in danger.

Chapter 6

"Who the hell is this immoral corrupt person? I'll stag him to death if I'll catch hold of him", shouted James. It was a really heartbreaking moment for him. He lost the person he loved. There was a kind of diverse expression on his face. He was neither angry nor melancholic nor expressed any other emotion that one is expected to show when he loses someone very dear to his heart. But his emotions confused everyone present there.

He yelled at the police and said, "Where is Stella Stewart?"

"Sir calm down."

"Where is she, just answer my question?"

"Behave yourself Mr. or else you'll be behind the bars."

"Shut up you bastard."

James started smacking the policemen one by one and completely lost his temper all of a sudden. The people gathered over there were startled by his reaction. Four of the policemen caught him, slapped him hard and locked him behind the bars."

One of them said, “Now stay there for a night you rascal. People like you deserve to be behind the bars.”

James shouted out angrily, “Where is Stella? I’m asking for the last time.”

Second one replied, “That’s none of your business.”

“It is my goddamn business you jerk. I’m sure enough that she is involved in this murder.”

“How can you be so sure?”

“Just call her right now.”

The policeman called another one and ordered him to get me to the police station immediately. The policeman reached my mansion and ordered me to follow him and took me to the police station where I heard James yelling out my name. I went up to him to have a talk with him and to know what’s going on. The policemen left us alone.

I asked, “What’s the matter James? Why are you yelling out my name like that and why did you call me over here?”

He replied,” Stop acting like an innocent woman, you two-faced cat. Tell me the reason for killing the Serena.”

I was astonished and shouted, “Are you nuts? Do you really think that I will kill my best friend?”

“I know it is you. You are a very crafty slayer. I don’t believe you.”

“You have to believe me. I have something to tell you. I know the person who’s behind all this.”

Our conversation carried on for an hour. After an hour the policeman called me back.

“James I have to leave but don’t you worry about anything. I’ll get you out of this lockup and then we’ll plan out something.”

“Take care Stella and beware.”

"Bye."

"Bye."

I went to one of the policemen and requested him to leave James. But he told me to get fifteen thousand dollars if I want to take him along right now else I should wait till tomorrow morning. I decided to wait for him till tomorrow morning.

I went to my residence. When I entered my bedroom I was terrified. There was a note written for me with blood on the mirror. It mentioned <u>I told you not to inform about this to anyone but you didn't listen. Now that you have gone against my warning you'll have to bear the consequences. If you can save him do it immediately before it's too late. If this time you'll inform anyone then my next target will be…..</u>

Without wasting much time I rushed to the police station. I inquired about James and I was informed that a person got him bailed and took him away. I asked them the person's name and physical features they just informed me that the person did not mention his name and he was wearing black sunglasses and hat so his face was not much visible. I told them that James's life might be at a risk. They immediately went out to search for him and after two hours while I was weeping they reported to me that he was dead and brutally slaughtered to death. I fell on the floor and wailed.

"But how did you know that his life was at a risk?"

I hesitated to tell them because I was not sure whether it would be correct to inform them or not.

"Miss Stella Stewart I suppose that I've asked you a question. I want you to answer right now."

"I felt something was wrong and so I told you."

"Really, stop lying to us. We are not fools."

"If you want you can search my house but don't doubt at me. As it is I've lost too many people this year."

"I'm sorry ma'am. Please you may leave."

"Thank you."

I left the police station and reached my homestead again. I found the mirror in bedroom was spotlessly clean and shining. I realized that somebody knows what I do each and every minute and keeps an eye on me. I must be alert now. But I fail to understand that how does he manage to do that. Once I'll trace out his secret route then I'll get to know who that person is. I noticed a chit under my feet. I picked it up and read so you didn't obey. This time I won't spare you bitch."

A minute later my cell phone started to vibrate and the screen flashed unknown number. I received the call. It was the same stranger.

He said in a forbidding tone, "Your friend James died due to your fault. Now Rey will also die. Hahahahhahahahah….."

I cried, "Please don't do any harm to him. It's a request. I'll do anything to rectify my mistake. Please forgive me and I assure you that this won't be repeated ever."

"But do you really assure that you'll be able to manage the task that would be laid upon you?"

"I can do anything to save his life. Bring it on."

After an hour a man entered my bedroom and we discussed the plan that I was commanded to inform him. We had to communicate to each other in such a manner that it appears as if we are lovers. Fifteen minutes later I heard Rey's footsteps walking upstairs.

I shouted out as loud as I could, "I know my love. He is a fool. I was with him for the sake of reputation and status. Now that you have entered my life I don't need him anymore. Rey thought that I was in love with him."

The man started giggling aloud with me. Suddenly the door slammed and opened and Rey looked at me disappointed. He was completely disheartened when he heard the entire conversation. He did not even bother to see the person I had communicated to and rushed downstairs as fast as his feet could carry him.

I ran after him and shouted, "Rey, stop right now."

He yelled at me, "So Miss Stella, now I know what your business is."

I cried, "What do you mean? Rey even you know that I'm not…"

"Not a word. It is my fault that I fell in love with a lady like you."

"Rey you are crossing your line."

"Which line Stella? If you can cross your line then why can't I?"

"Of course you can but only till the time you don't interfere in my life. Whatever I do, with whom I stay, whom I love, etc, should not bother you. You are neither my boyfriend nor a friend nor a husband that you are questioning me like that."

"I'm actually your no one."

"Thank God you finally realized that. Listen to me Rey, get the hell out of my house right now and don't you dare enter my house ever again without my permission."

"Who the hell wants to enter again? I am breaking up with you."

"You are seriously a crazy man. How can you break up with me when we are not even in a relationship? I think that you must consult a psychiatrist. I know one. May I fix an appointment for you?"

"No thanks. Goodbye Stella."

"Thank you for leaving."

"Enjoy your night with that bastard."

"I will. So please will you leave."

"Sure."

He just stared me for a second and I could see that his eyes were full of rage. He left broken. I was sorry but I will apologize to him once I sort things out. I wonder that why did the person, who was here, escaped when he saw Rey? Maybe I'll get a clue. I searched for the clue everywhere within my entire house but I could not find anything. Then I went inside my washroom. I found the clue there. I was surprised that the person dared to enter even my washroom. A small paper was lying on the basin.

It was written <u>I was the one who informed Rey about your performance over here. Actually my main aim was not to force you to fuck anyone but to break your heart. You should thank me since I made your task easier. Now Rey would loathe you forever. You are all alone. Enjoy the night because this night would be the last joyful night of your life,</u>

This time I was too annoyed that I bellowed out, "Who are you and why the hell are you after my life? If you have the grit come and face me else I would declare you with the title of a donkey."

I was actually felt downcast at these hours of darkness. I could not disclose this secret to anyone so I engraved all my emotions and enigmas in my diary. I then felt like thumping someone and so I grabbed a pumic stone hardly in my left fist and threw it at the mirror. What I saw after that changed my life forever.

Chapter 7

"Rey it's been two years we've been married. But it seems as if you don't care for me. Answer me frankly today, do you really love me?" inquired Kimaya.

Rey replied hesitatingly, "Stop asking me foolish questions."

"That's not the answer to my question Rey."

"I love you. Satisfied now, let me go else I'll be reprimanded by my chief."

"I won't let you leave like that. You are lying to me. I know you still have feelings for Stella."

"I told you I don't have time for all this you dumb woman."

"That means you still love him. I'm not imprudent that you can fool me anytime you feel like. I'm not the kind of a woman you can just operate and later discard. I have certain self-esteem. I am not a product that will expire. For heaven sake I am your spouse and you better treat me like one."

"Don't irritate me or I'll slap you hard silly."

"So it's come to this. You better stay within your limits. If you really love me then prove it to me."

"I don't feel it important to prove you anything right now."

"Rey you can't leave me like that. So Stella is the problem."

"She's not the cross you are the one. You are ruining our married life. I'm leaving now."

"Rey I won't irritate you only if you'll kiss me once. If you'll kiss me, you'll prove it to me that you are only mine."

"If that is the condition then I'll kiss you and leave."

Kimaya stroked her arms around his waist and pulled him closer. She then bent forward to kiss him. Rey paused in the middle of their kiss and pushed him backwards.

"Why did you stop?"

"I did what you told me to. I've proved you that I'm doted to you. Kimaya it's getting late now. Bye."

After he left, Kimaya rushed to her room and wept for a while. She then told herself "So you've proved me that you still love that bitch. I will kill her. Even though she's not married to you yet she's interfering indirectly in my married life and I can't take it anymore. I curse you Stella. You'll die soon for filching Rey forcefully. I hate you for this."

While Rey was absorbed in his work a thought struck in his mind Kimaya is right. Why do I still feel for her? She was disloyal, she was the one who used me even then why do I sense that something is erroneous in all that I saw and heard? No Rey focus. You are married now. You must love only Kimaya and not Stella. Just obliterate her out of your life Rey.

A few seconds later his cell rang and he received the call. It was Kimaya.

She shouted gladly, "Rey I have a lovely news for you. Stella Stewart is dead. She is finally dead."

"What? No, this can't be true. Stop teasing me. It's not funny. She can't die."

"Why are you sounding so depressed? I thought that you hated her."

"I hate her still, but I never wished that to happen to her."

"Rey calm down. It's the breaking news of every news channel today."

Rey could not feel anything at that moment. He dropped his cell and it broke. He immediately switched on the television and watched the news channel.

The reporter said, "Miss Stella Stewart, a young woman of about 23 years old, died this morning. She was a millionaire. She had committed a suicide. It was proved by the suicide letter that she wrote before committing suicide. Now I'll read the suicide note <u>I was happy with my married life. Robert loved me more than I ever deserved. I love him too but I was not worth this care and concern. I was an actor not by profession but an actor who earned her living by committing to men. As soon as I would receive their luxuries I would break their heart and leave them forever. Robert was the first guy I fell in love with. I was a voracious woman and I loved wealth more than him. I always thirsted for money and luxuries. One day I felt that I was wrong and deceiving the person who loved me so much. Before I could leave to tell him the truth I got the news that he committed a suicide when he discovered the truth himself. I was utterly culpable and so I decided to die because death is the only solution to rectify all my mistakes and I can't live without him. So</u>

here I consider myself as defeated and so it's a goodbye. Stella Stewart.

After the reports it has been proved that this letter is original. The handwriting in this matches that with Stella's. The investigation is still carried on. The policemen still suspected that Stella has not committed a suicide but has been brutally assassinated. Three years back three murders took place in the similar pattern. They all had strong connections with Stella. One of them was her own mother, Julie Stewart. Two others were her best friend, Serena Jaitley, and Serena's boyfriend, James Mcallister. The DNA and forensic reports clearly indicate that the criminal behind all these murders is the same. Stella's corpse went for further investigation."

Rey was completely startled after hearing the news report. He could not believe what he heard. He was not prepared to judge me as infidel. Lastly, he could not believe that I was dead. He was in a state of limbo. Though he was alive yet he felt that he died along with me. This is true love. Despite of all I did to him his heart knew that something is wrong and he wanted to discover it. He was all geared up to help the cops in this investigation but Kimaya called him and laid a condition before him that if you want to go against my will and get involved in this investigation then you must divorce me first. After Kimaya's call, Rey was disturbed and finally took a resolute that he will erase Stella's memories forever and would not get drawn in any sort of investigation.

That night he premeditated on how to conquer Kimaya's heart. She was the one who has always been just, loving and loyal to him. He deliberately wanted to apologize to her and initiate their marriage with love and only love. He went to a jeweler's shop and bought an exquisite diamond ring for her. He then bought a 2 pounds truffle cake for her and a bouquet of red roses.

While he was seated in a cab, he rang Kimaya and requested her to leave the house for an hour, pleading a surprise for her. When he reached home he went to his living room and made all the preparations to surprise her. After an hour he turned off all the lights and waited outside for her. A few minutes later he saw a cab and he knew that it was Kimaya. Before she could enter the house he covered her eyes with a blindfold and requested her to follow. He took her to the living room and opened her blindfold.

It was the best surprise of Kimaya's life. She was shocked that Rey made all the preparations for her. The room was lit with red lights and red lanterns. She could scent the sweet smell of vanilla candles floating over a huge bowl filled with water. The walls consisted of collages full of their pictures. A huge silver banner was hanging above in which was written in broad letters KIMAYA I LOVE YOU.

She said, "Rey thank you so much. This is the best surprise of my life. How much I desired you to love me like this? Finally you are mine."

"I was always yours lady, I was so stupid that I never realized it before. I'm sorry Kimaya for hurting you always and thanks for being compassionate to me always."

"You always deserved it. Forget the past and cheer up now."

"Wait."

He took out the box of ring from his pocket and opened it. He took the bouquet of roses and said, "Here Kimaya accept it."

She took the bouquet and kept it aside. Rey held Kimaya's hands and said, "Kimaya I love you. Will you be my soulmate?"

"Of course I will. You don't know how much I longed to hear these three words from your mouth. I love you too."

Rey slid the ring through her fourth finger and she kissed it. He then lifted her and carried her to the bedroom. He dropped her gently over the bed and he too fell above her. He kissed her and their lips locked embracing each other. There appeared an expression of conquest on Kimaya's face the every time Rey kissed him. They made love the entire night.

Next day Rey was fell too tired to go anywhere. Seeking the advantage of the fact, Kimaya insisted him to stay at home, to which he agreed. Around nine in the morning she got two cups of coffee. They had a long conversation that day.

Everything changed day by day. They both spent most of their time together and Rey felt as if he's got his life back. A year passed by and Stella was no more a part of his life now. He uttered out only Kimaya's name every moment of his life and he became conscious about the definition of true love.

Though he had no issues with his life now yet it is always said that past repeats itself at some stage of a person's life. Rey could not escape from that and has to admit that he can't stay away from me for a longer time.

One night he had a terrible nightmare which opened his eyes. In his nightmare he saw my corpse hung by a rope tied around my neck and I was full of blood. The sight of my dead body was sickening and it aroused him. He trembled with fear the rest of the night.

Next day also he felt too restless. He sat numbly at work wandering what the dream signified the previous night. Suddenly the whole past appeared before him like a flashback and he was engrossed in it.

Chapter 8

I was busy circulating the invitation cards of my marriage ceremony. It was after three days. I was marrying Robert Patrick against my will. Everybody was jovial after receiving the invitation except for one. I left the last invitation for Rey. After I distributed the invitation to everyone I went up to Rey and handed him the invitation and was about to leave when he asked me to stop.

"Wait Stella. You never revealed it to anyone that you are marrying a person whom you don't even know. Is he offering you enough wealth?"

"Rey I love him and so I'm marrying him."

"I thought you don't know the definition of love."

"I'm not in a mood to discuss this with you. Nobody in this world can describe love better than me."

"This is the biggest joke of the year. Your life itself mocks at you presently. So what according to you is love? Oh! Whom am I asking this? According to you love is wealth."

"Love is selfish. It's all consuming and full of forfeit. The one who's in love hands over her life to her beloved eternally and can go to any extent to save the person she loves. A lady who once falls in love with a man bestows all her happiness to her beloved one. A lady can love a man to such an extent that she can even sacrifice her own mirth for him. Despite of all her sacrifices she only gets pain and misery in return."

After I completed, the atmosphere was still and silent. We stared each other for around five minutes but when I felt that I'm giving him false signals I rolled my eyes and left the spot. I rushed hurriedly towards my cab waiting outside the college entrance gate. Before I could get inside the cab somebody grabbed my arm and pulled me back. I thought that it was Rey and so I roared out loud, "Stop it Rey."

When I looked back, it he was not Rey but Robert. I said, "Rob, you are here?"

"Why? Do I need an appointment to visit my fiancée now? I was missing you and so I came over here to meet you."

"Stop pretending and just tell me what are you doing over here? When I already said that I will be back soon then who told you to leave the place where you were?"

"Stella, calm down babes. Won't you introduce me to your friends? Even if you don't wish to, you have to, you don't have a choice."

"Just leave. Don't create a scene over here."

He clutched my right arm and forcefully led me back into the college campus where everyone was eager to know that who was the guy with me.

Robert announced, "Hi everyone, I am Robert Patrick, Stella's fiancée. Pleased to meet you all. I stand here to announce that I and Stella are getting married after three days and I want each and every student present in this campus to attend our grand wedding. It will be one of the best wedding ever."

Pridella shouted gladly, "Rob we'll be there positively."

Saira said, "Stella you are propitious to have a life partner like him. Look at him. He's so scorching and debonair. I just could not stop staring you. There is not even a single woman in this world I think who can reject him. I wish I was at your place."

I thought if you want to take my place you are most welcome. At least I'll get rid of him and his pranks. Please take my place and set me free.

My thoughts were interrupted by Saira, "Stella, where are you lost? By the way congratulations to both of you."

Robert replied, "Thank you everyone."

Robert was walking in my direction. I wandered what was he up to now? Before I could think of anything else he leaned forward and kissed me, brushing my lips. How awkward I felt, kissing the person I abhor the most before the entire college. He kissed me continuously for a few minutes and then stepped backwards. Unfortunately, I found Rey staring at me, his eyes filled with tears rolling out in a flow. When I saw him grieved I was about to weep to when I controlled my emotions and wiped my tears before they could flow out and indicate my true intentions to him.

Robert noticed me staring at Rey and so he wrapped his arms around my waist and pulled me in his direction. I whispered in his ears, "It was not included anywhere. Stop messing up the situation and leave."

He whispered, "You just can't do anything. I love humiliating you before your lover."

He went up to Rey and said, "I've heard a lot about you to Rey. Stella really considers you as a friend who is close to her heart. ONLY AND ONLY A FRIEND."

Rey replied, "I don't consider her even as a friend. Congratulations, you are really lucky."

"I know that. Thanks for telling anyways. Stella wanted you to attend our wedding. So you'll be there, right."

"I won't be able to reach there. I'm busy this weekend. I don't have time for all this shit."

"But I insist you to come. Stella request him to come."

"Rey if you won't come then I'll believe that you still...."

"I'll be there."

"Stella, please leave both of us alone for sometime. I want talk to him in private."

"Sure."

I left them alone but I speculated on what were his intentions next. I decided to secretly hear their conversation and so I hid myself behind the bark of a huge banyan tree and listened.

Robert said, "Your face clearly depicts that you love her still."

"No I don't, and how do you know about this? Nobody in this college knows that."

"I am aware of each and every thing that happens in her life. I am a kind of a satellite who follows her everywhere."

"Listen, what I feel and what I don't, should not concern you. Just leave me alone."

"Poor love bird. Do you think that even she loves you? Let me notify you that she only loves me and will not dare to love anyone else."

"We'll see whom she loves and whom she does not after three days. I'm sure she'll come back to me soon."

"Let's wait till then. Wish you all the very best."

"Same to you."

Before Robert gets to know that I heard their conversation, I secretly left them and sat inside my cab. After two minutes Rob entered and ordered the driver to go home. He kept his hand over mine but I resisted.

"Don't mix business with pleasures. How dare you kiss me?"

"Just shut up. Why the hell did you listen to our conversation?"

I panicked. How did he know that? I answered hesitatingly, "I don't know what you're talking about?"

"Stop fibbing and reply."

He seized my hair and heaved it. I yelled with anguish. I requested him to leave. After few seconds he set them free and I moved backwards.

"Don't be afraid of me. I won't harm you anyhow. I just want to seek revenge. I want to make your life hell. I would mess your life to such an extent that you'll only desire to die rather than leading such a miserable life."

"What's next?"

"First marry me and then you'll get to know. Why are you becoming so impatient. You have to spend your whole life with me now. So be patient."

"You won't get anything by doing all this."

"You're wrong. I'll get self-satisfaction."

"Bullshit."

He dropped me home and warned me not to act sly because he will take a measure if I'll go against his commands. This time I didn't follow.

Robert entered the 'City Night Club' and was sat at the beer counter waiting in joyful anticipation for the arrival of someone. He ordered four glasses of icy vodkas and drank them. An hour passed by but there was no sign of the person he was waiting for. He kept on ordering vodkas one by one and gulping them at a great speed. He finished almost eight bottles of vodka, yet there was no sign of that person.

Three hours passed by and the person he was waiting for finally arrived. She was none other but Kimaya. Robert had called her there. But he was not in his senses to talk. Kimaya, with the assistance of two other men, carried him to the cab and Kimaya instructed her driver to drop them home. Kimaya opened the door and managed somehow with her driver's help to make him lie down on her bed. She slept on the couch that night.

The next morning, Robert was astonished to find himself lying in an unknown place. When he went out of the room he saw Kimaya lying on the couch and sleeping peacefully. He went up to her and woke her up.

"Why do you consume so much of alcohol when lose your senses after that. You created such a chaos last night."

He lifted his right hand and tickled her shoulders with his fingers and slid them sideways. Kimaya tugged his hand.

"Rob, have a control over your intentions and don't you lay hand on me like that again or else I'll forget everything and…."

"I'm sorry, I won't repeat it. You know how much I love you."

"You are sick. I'm not with you over here for getting into a relationship with you. Just tell me what you want and get going."

"Do you know what Rey answered me? He still loves her."

"Dammm, can't you have a control over your girlfriend. If she steals my boyfriend then I'll threaten both of you after that. You better be mindful of that."

"She's completely under my control. She'll only do as instructed to her by me."

"I still can't overlook the day when she kissed my Rey. The three of us implemented out a dinner party one night, though I refused to be a part of that, later I decided to surprise them. But what I perceived after when I reached Stella's residence was not at all acceptable. She embittered me. She knew very well that I loved him. I detest that bitch."

"How did you feel when he proposed you?"

"I am aware that it was just a co-incidence. He wanted to propose Stella. I don't care whether it was unreal or not, what matters is that he proposed me and he can't leave me now, else it would ruin his reputation. I was about to leave that night when I met you and you gave me such a brilliant initiative that Stella rejected his proposal that day."

"I remember, I suggested you to give her a prank call."

"Yeah, I called her that night and changed my tone and spoke to her. I said that Stella if you'll accept Rey's proposal then his life may be in danger. And she like a fool believed me."

"Don't give yourself too much credit. After that I was the one who handled the whole situation."

"How did you manage to convince her that Rey's life would be in danger? Why did she believe you and why did you asked me to leave while you were communicating with her?"

"It's incompetent to answer all these questions. You've got your Rey that's sufficient."

"All thanks to you Robert. May I ask you one last question?"

"Just one."

"Why are you marrying Stella when you abhor her? Why did you help me out? Why do you love me despite knowing I love Rey?"

"Yes, I love you but I dislike her more than I like you. Once I'll settle all my scores with her then I'll be back. I suppose I've answered your question. May I take a leave now?"

"Thanks for laying a helping hand on me."

"Anytime lady. I'm there to assist you always. I'm sure you'll manage further. Take care Kimaya."

"Can we be friends?"

"I don't believe in friendship. If you can love me then surely I'm yours."

"Forget it then."

"Bye. See you tomorrow in the church."

"How can I miss my best friend's and my best enemy's marriage? I'll be there positively."

"I hope you remember your part. You know how you have to tackle the whole situation tomorrow? Try persuading him to marry you tomorrow."

"I will."

"Good luck."

Chapter 9

All the people were seated inside the church. Everyone was full of zest waiting eagerly for me and Robert. After some time me and Robert entered and all the eyes were on us. We stood before priest where he proceeded with the ceremony. I realized that James was not there and I did not want him to be there.

Father said, "Do you, Robert Patrick, accept Stella Stewart as your lawfully wedded wife?"

He gave me one of those weird looks and replied with a filthy smile, "I do."

He then faced me and asked, "Do you, Miss Stella Stewart, accept Robert Patrick as your lawfully wedded husband?"

Before I could answer I saw James standing before my eyes, hoping that I might refuse to marry Rob. There was complete silence around and all eyes were on me.

With a deep breath I replied, "I.....I do."

I looked into James's eyes, he looked into mine. I could observe the anger filled in his eyes to burn the error that I made in the statement. I could feel the beating of his heart shouting out loud to accept him back and love him.

Father shouted, "Congratulations, you both are a couple now. Dear son you may now kiss the bride."

I thought please no, not again. I hate kissing him. His breath is foul, his touch is foul. He himself is foul. Please leave James. I can't kiss before him. I want to get out of this mess.

I said, "Father, please can I take a leave. I'm not well. I don't want my newly wedded husband to be ill too."

Robert held my hand and said, "It's a custom. You can't change it."

Father replied, "No my child. You may leave if you want to."

"Thank you father."

Before Robert could create a scene I rushed out and wept loudly. Suddenly somebody placed his arm over my shoulder. I turned back to retaliate. Then I stopped. It was James.

I said, "James, please leave me alone today. I'm not in a mood to…"

He shouted, "Shut up. Who the hell wants to speak to you? You are a selfish and egocentric lady. You are a bitch in disguise of a lady."

"Don't speak to me like that."

"Why do you appear as if you are so melancholic? Just stop this fake pretence of yours."

"I'm not counterfeiting."

"Let it be. Congratulations, you are married now."

"Thanks."

"Don't want to see you ever again. I want to curse you, but I won't."

"You are not doing any favor by doing so."

"Now it's your turn to congratulate me."

"What?"

"Wait, I'll be back within a few seconds."

He went inside the church and returned back. He was not alone. Kimaya accompanied him too.

James stood before me and held Kimaya's hand. He kissed her palm and asked, "Kimaya, will you marry me?"

There was a big glow in her face. She smiled and replied, "Of course I will."

"Now."

"Sure."

"Congratulations", shouted out a voice. It was Robert. He came forward and embraced me.

"Sweetheart let's go home."

"Yeah."

Kimaya stopped me and with a pierce look said, "Stella you can't leave. You must attend our wedding too."

"I'm tired."

"Common."

Robert said, "Kimaya, don't force her. Wish you both a very happy married life in advance. We have to catch a flight tomorrow. So we need to pack our stuff."

Kimaya said, "You never told us that you both are leaving tomorrow. But why are you going so soon?"

"We have to leave urgently due to certain family problems."

"When are you planning to return?"

"Never."

"What?"

"I want to take her away from, I hope you understand."

James shouted out loud, "What do you mean?"

He replied, "You know very well. Don't provoke me to utter out everything."

Kimaya said, "Just stop both of you. Take it easy."

Robert said, "We are leaving now. Goodbye."

James said, "Kimaya I don't have time for all this. Let's get married and leave."

Kimaya said, "James I need to speak to Stella alone."

"Okay, I'm waiting inside."

"I'm waiting for you outside."

"Okay Rob."

I saw James for the last time because I knew that it was the end of all. He left. After a few seconds even Robert left.

Chapter 10

"Rey, wake up. It's nine. You'll be late otherwise."

"I'm awake."

"Breakfast is ready."

"Just give me a few minutes, Kimaya."

"Rey don't leave today. Stay at home with me."

"I have to go. I'm piled up with a lot of work nowadays."

"Fine, I'm waiting in the living room. You know I hate waiting for a long time. I'm very impatient."

"Me too."

While Rey was waiting he was mesmerized in our past memories. He spoke to himself, "Last night also you came in my dreams. Why are you after my life Stella? I want to forget you forever. I want to live happily with Kimaya. Though you are dead but somewhere I feel that what I heard is untrue. You are alive. Rey what's the matter and why am I bothered about all this? She was the one who embittered me. Just overlook everything or I'll slap myself hard."

He heard Kimaya calling out his name. He wiped his body with a towel gently and after dressing up went to Kimaya. She went forward to kiss him.

"I told you I hate waiting."

"Kimaya where is my breakfast, I have to leave."

"What's the matter baby, you look really disturbed. Why do you sound so grief-stricken? Tell me."

"Nothing."

"Don't try my patience now", she shouted out loud, "You still love her. Stop double crossing me. I won't bear it any more. Rey open your eyes. She dumped you long back. She's dead. I wish she was dead before meeting you. At least I would have got rid of the nuisance."

Rey slapped her and roared, "Don't you dare talk to me like that again. You have no right to speak ill about her."

"You slapped me for that moron. Get lost you bastard."

Suddenly Rey came back to his senses and cried, "I'm sorry Kimaya. I didn't intend to hurt you. I'm not well. I'll stay at home today."

"Rey you've crossed the line today. I don't want to talk to you."

"I apologized to you. Kimaya I'm taking you out for a date. It's been long time since we have chilled out together."

"Don't change the topic. I'm upset."

"Are you sure?"

She embraced him and said, "Let's go. I can't ignore you. Love you."

"Love you too."

I was swinging on the rocking chair. My entire body was like a carcass. I was dead to live my life. I just hope that Rey has forgotten me. I was disturbed by a bang at my door. Robert was yelling out my name. I didn't reply. He broke the door and entered with thud. He grabbed my arm and pulled my hair. I screamed in agony.

"Robert it's hurting."

"Next time when I call out your name reply me at once else I'll torment you more."

"Leave me I say."

He withdrew his hands.

I said, "I did everything as you've planned. According to the entire world I'm dead but only we know that I'm alive. But why did you plan this fake death of mine?"

"I did so coz I don't want your romeo boyfriend to look for you."

"What next?"

"Before executing my next plan make sure that nobody recognizes you. From today onwards your name is Rose."

"What is the need to change my name?"

"So that nobody identifies you. I'll take care of the passports. Well I'm giving you a chance to get rid of all this and go back to your boyfriend. I'll give you a task and if you manage to complete it successfully I'll spare your life and Rey's also."

"What's the task?"

"Let me complete. You have two options. First one is to complete this task. But the twist is that if you'll fail in the task, you'll be hung to death. Second option is that you stay with me and let me harass you. At least you'll be alive in this. Choose wisely."

"I go with the first one. Bring it on."

"As you say, this is what I love about you. I love this attitude of yours. It befits you completely. You never lose hope. Oh my! Your overconfidence will definitely kill you one day."

"I suppose that we are not present over here to discuss my pros and cons. Be brief and let me know what's in your mind. I know you very well. You'll tell me tomorrow. So I'm going off to sleep."

"Bingo. I think we make a perfect match. Why don't you stay with me for the rest of your life? If you'll support me once then we both will rule over the whole universe."

"No thanks, as I've mentioned before, I don't mix business with pleasures. Rob, countdown begins. Let me get out of here once and then I'll ruin your life."

He laughed wildly. "Oh my God! I'm scared of you. Miss Stella, sorry, Rose, you are a loser and dumb woman. Planning and plotting is not your cup of tea."

"You don't know me yet."

"We'll see later."

"Anyways, wish you a very horrifying night. I truly desire that every dream of yours will choke you to death."

"In your dreams only I can have such a miserable dream. For now, don't forget that you are under my control. So talk less and work more."

"I am doing so already."

"Good night to you."

"Your good wishes are not required."

It was midnight and I was feeling restless. I faced Robert and after confirming that he was sleeping soundly I rose up silently and went to the balcony.

I whispered to myself, "Robert I've had enough. Let me first search for what I want to, after that I'll slander you. I must search for the documents, videos and pictures before he wakes up. Let me confirm again whether he is actually asleep or just pretending. I opened the door slightly and heard Robert snoring. He was asleep. This is the best opportunity I could ever get. I must not waste it. He usually does not sleep and wakes up even if he is disturbed by a pin drop. I was aware of it and this is the reason that made me evil. I added sleeping pills in his drink which he gulped delightfully. Now he won't disrupt me till morning. I must hurry now."

That night was the last opportunity of mine to escape. I searched for the clues in every nook and corner of the house like a rat. While I was on my way, the door slam opened and Robert entered. I was traumatized with fear.

"Searching for the clue? You won't get it ever. I saw you when you were blending those sleeping pills in my drink. So I changed the drink while you were outside. I was pretending to sleep. I just wanted to see you in action. As I've said before also that you are a loser. So let's sleep now."

"I might have failed today but I'll be careful next time."

"Hahahaahhaahaaaaaa. We'll see then. If you'll delay more I'll deduct one day."

"One day. I didn't get it."

"In short, I won't inform you about the plan."

"Good night."

Chapter 11

Rey was waiting for the policeman. He was in the police station. He was called for inquiry.

The officer said, "I'm inspector Robert Decoster. Sorry to keep you waiting. So tell me that what was your relation with Miss Stella Stewart in past and enlighten me with all the information about her."

He replied, "I used to love her, and I think that I still love her."

He narrated the whole incident to him and all that he spoke was getting recorded in a device for future investigations. He informed him that how I dumped him and married Robert and under what circumstances he married Kimaya.

"I'm really sorry about all this. Don't you think that something is fishy. I fail to understand that why did she reject you suddenly? You also told me that Kimaya was her best friend. Stella knew that she liked you too. It's enigmatic."

"I don't know. I've lost all my senses after that incident. Maybe my expectations from life were too high. I'm satisfied with my life now. I love Kimaya."

"You know it better that you have feelings for her."

"I'm confused."

"You may leave now. I'll call you again whenever required. Thanks for the information."

"Anytime."

Rey was walking across the street almost lost. His ears turned deaf to the hoots and noise around. He could only hear the words spoken by the officer. They were echoing in his mind like a tape of a cassette 'You know it better that you have feelings for her.' When he reached home Kimaya was not there. She went for a party. He was relieved that she was not there else she would have irritated him with numerous questions.

He whispered to himself 'I'm sick and tired of all this. I think I need a break. I'll take Kimaya to Paris for a vacation. No Rey, no, it's not the time to run away from all this. I must have the courage to face all this. Within every beat of my heart I could only hear Stella's name. My life is linked with hers. Somewhere I feel that she is still alive and my mother, when I was young, has always taught me not to come to any conclusions without any proof. I must search her house and look for her for the last time.'

Without wasting any more time, he instructed the driver to drop him before Stella's former house. He was sure that he can get a clue there. He called Kimaya once to make sure that she does not interfere later in the middle of his search.

Unfortunately, when he reached there, the flap was locked. He looked for another route to enter, and he found that a window was open. He managed to climb and enter through it. He carried on with his pursuit. After three hour he got hold of a diary. It was my personal diary. He was mesmerized by its occurrence. He took the diary and went back. He entered without a sound to make sure that if Kimaya is inside, she won't notice him hiding the diary. She was yet out. So he hurried to his room and hid the diary inside the wooden cupboard of his room. After thirty minutes Kimaya came and called for Rey. He hugged her.

"Where were you? I was waiting for you. I want to hang out with you. It's been a long time. So I've decided to plan a trip to Paris."

"Sounds amazing. Love you baby."

"Kimaya I'm really pissed off today so please do me a favor? Can you go and book two tickets?"

"With pleasure, anything for you. I'll just leave after an hour or two."

"No, leave right now else we won't get the tickets by today. I don't want to miss this opportunity. I've already taken a leave of two weeks from my office."

"You care so much for me. I'll be back then. I'm leaving for now. I'll get the bookings done and then we'll have fun tonight."

After she left, he went upstairs and took out the diary. He opened it gradually and flipped the pages as he read them. Every word that he read made him shed tears and yell at himself. He discovered that she loved him too.

'Guess what? Rey proposed me today. He made my evening. I used to hate him when I met him for the first time. As time passed by I started liking him. His smile is really a cute one. He is tremendously hot. I can never get my eyes off him. I know that Kimaya loves him too. I'm stuck between love and friendship. I love you Rey and I've finally decided to be yours forever. I was about to accept his proposal but that call messed up everything and.....'

"Honey I'm back", shouted Kimaya, "Where are you? Are you upstairs? Stay there. I'm coming."

Rey hid the diary again and after a few minutes Kimaya stroked her arms around his chest and embraced him from the back.

"Kimaya, you are back, so soon."

"Why are you asking me such a question? I thought you wanted me to spend time with you alone. This is the reason why I rushed. I got the tickets. The good news is that we are departing tomorrow. Isn't it incredible?"

"That's great. Can you pack my stuff too? I am going off to sleep."

"Sure. Goodnight."

"Goodnight."

Rey lay on the bed and pretended to sleep. He thought "I must read the diary completely before we leave tomorrow. Stella I must know that why did you reject me when you love me? As soon as Kimaya falls asleep I'll read the diary."

"Good morning Stella", shouted Rob.

"Get lost. Don't want to see your face early in the morning else you'll ruin my whole day."

"Very funny. Just wake up. I don't like talking to losers like you. I'm waiting outside. Pace up."

I rose up and dressed up as soon as possible. I was sure that he will discuss his plan. This was the chance to save my love and life. I was well prepared.

Rey, after corroborating that Kimaya was asleep, rose up and went to the living room along with the diary. He opened it again and started reading from where he had paused last time and it solved one-fourth of the case.

Dear diary,

Now I'll tell you the reason of my rejection. I wanted to dedicate my entire life to Rey. I want to marry him. I wanted to make that moment eternal, when we kissed for the first time. I received a call from a stranger today. His voice was hoarse. He said, "Don't ask me any questions and listen to me very carefully. You must reject Rey's proposal. You have to humiliate him." I asked, "Who are you and how dare you command me like that?"

He replied, "I told you no questions. I want to tell you a reality about your lover. I am the one who is responsible for your mom's death. Yes, I am the devil you are looking for since such a long duration. But you won't be able to prove this. When I killed your mother mercilessly, no one was around, except for Rey. Luckily he was not able to get hold of me and he even could not see my face because I my face was covered by a black mask. He chased me but all in vain. Then he went up to your mother's corpse and he thought that I had escaped. But I didn't. I was hidden somewhere behind the bushes.

While he held your mother in his arms I clicked pictures, and he even lifted the murder weapon in which his fingerprints were traced. I still have the reports.

In brief, all proofs are against him and the cops are still in search of the mysterious murderer. If I'll send these pictures to the police station they'll arrest him. I hope you are aware that people only believe in proofs. You can only save your boyfriend from death if you'll do as I instruct. You won't be able to get any clue against me because things were pre-planned and since it is my plan it is perfect."

After that he laughed like a devil and disconnected the call. I was trapped. I had no option but to reject him. I wish I could apologize to him once.

Rey was grief-stricken after he read each word. This time he moaned without a pause, shedding huge tears of guilt in a continuous flow. He whispered to himself, "I'm sorry Stella. I never imagined that you love me so much. I'm going to kill that bastard. I am responsible for your death and I'm sure now that you are still alive. I won't be able to forgive myself for the rest of my life if I won't be able to save you this time."

He flipped the page in hope to get another clue. Unfortunately, that was the last page that he had read. After that what happened, I did not write.

He shouted irritatingly. He then went to the room silently and hid the diary. He went off to sleep.

Chapter 12

"Welcome Stella, please take a seat. It's raining heavily. Isn't it an extremely romantic weather? I feel like……"

"Stop talking gibberish and tell me about your plan. Be brief, as I know very well that you talk rubbish."

"Impressive."

"Mind you, I'm not in a mood of all this. So please don't get on my nerves and come straight to the point. If you want to talk about all this shit then I'm leaving."

"Oh my God! You are too arrogant."

"Just shut up now, else I'll leave immediately."

"Alright, my plan is this. We are going to execute the biggest robbery ever known to this world. Sorry for the error, you alone will be raiding. I will only assist you and instruct you. But mind it, if you are caught, you'll be sentenced to a lifetime imprisonment."

"I'm all set for all this."

"You seriously seem to amaze me. You have a lot of guts."

"Give me the details of the robbery."

"First thing is first, are you in? Do you still want to risk your life? It's like a game of life. In this, either you'll gain everything or lose all."

"As I've mentioned before also that I'm geared up."

"Cool then. So here is the idea.

He continued discussing about the robbery and she continued to listen. It was absolutely a terrific task for her.

"Miss Stewart the plan must be executed in Paris. I will hand over a guide map of that complex to you."

"Which complex?"

"Stop playing KBC with me and let me finish. I'm telling you step by step."

"Carry on."

"There is a world famous MULTI- PURPOSE SELLENA COMPLEX in Paris. This is your venue. There are many shops within it. There is also a museum inside."

"You want me to get jewellery or stuff like that from those shops."

"Shut up before I lose my temper."

"Sorry."

"Inside the museum there is high tech security. You'll be given all the details in the guide map of museum. You have to cross them and steal the famous platinum statue of FLIP FLOP LADY. I'll send you the picture of that statue."

"Do you expect me to carry that heavy statue all by myself?"

"You ladies are seriously terrible. You just have to carry it outside the complex. The rest I'll manage."

"How will I lift such a heavy statue?"

"That's your problem, not mine. I will only let you free if you'll get me that statue. Its market value is around a hundred billion pounds in today's market."

"I need all the details immediately."

"Don't bother about that. I'll give you a cell and all the details will be mentioned in it. Mind it, you can only call me and attend my calls only. No incoming as well as outgoing. So don't try to act cunning."

"Do I have an option?"

"So are you in?"

With a deep breath I replied, "Let's go for it."

"Are you sure? You can still change your decision."

"My decision is final. Do you get that?"

"So we will execute the robbery after five days. Tomorrow we have to catch a flight to Paris."

After he left I thought that this is the last chance. I must get back and reciprocate Rey's love. I'll tell him everything and also need to warn him that her wife Kimaya is wicked as well as cunning. I wish I gain victory this time.

"Good morning Rey. We have to catch a flight after an hour. Are you done with all the packing? What a stupid question I'm asking, I was the one who packed your stuff."

"Let's leave, be quick. Can't delay today?"

"What's the difference in today and the rest of the days of the week?"

"I don't want to delay because.....because I want to spend time with you there in Paris."

"How sweet, come give me a kiss."

She was about to kiss when Rey stopped her. "Be patient, we need to catch a flight so we'll do all this later."

"Okay, I' m going upstairs."

After she left he murmured, "Phew, got rid of her. I won't cheat Stella and that's a promise. Stella where so ever in this world you are, I'm going to find you soon and then we'll be together again. I just hope that wherever you are for now, you are secure."

"Ready."

"Yes. Let's leave."

Chapter 13

We were on our way to Paris, seated in a flight. Coincidently, I and Rey were in the same flight and very close to each other. He was seated five rows ahead of me. Neither he was aware of it nor I.

Rey called for the air hostess and ordered a glass of icy vodka. He kept on ordering glasses of vodka and consuming them all in a single nip. He was completely unrestrained after consuming vodka and he lost consciousness and his senses after an hour. His weird acts mystified Kimaya.

"Rey, don't drink now."

"As you say, Stella, my love. Your wish is my command."

"Stella, are you out of your mind? I'm Kimaya your wife. Dare you utter out that person's name from your lips again."

He was frenzied. He muttered, "You dumb woman. Who told you to do a favor to me? You are a boyfriend moocher. You are a very self-obsessed, egoistic woman."

He rose up in complete rage and stumbled. She held him but he pushed her backwards. Everybody worried over what was going on as they were aware that the guy was crazy and under the influence of alcohol. It was a humorous scene for every passenger. I don't know why people find every conflict between a husband and a wife so interesting. The air hostess complained and pleaded him to be seated. He yelled at her instead and ordered her not to interfere.

He shouted out loud, "Stella I love you."

As soon as I heard someone yelling out my name and confessing his love for me I faced him. To my revulsion, that alcoholic person was Rey. I was anxious at his sudden appearance. I must be cautious. If he discovers that I'm alive, don't know what all consequences I have to face later. I just verified whether Robert has seen him or not. To my dismay, he had his eyes on him. I was trapped again.

Kimaya rose up too in annoyance and shrieked, "Stop all this right now. Sit down and sleep. You've lost it."

"You are right I've lost it. I've lost my senses the day I married you. You want to know the truth, so listen, I HATE YOU. Only one woman has a place in my hub and that's Stella. I was in love with her since the first day I met her. I've always been attracted to her. I'm in love with her million dollar smile, her pink and lusty lips, her deep brown, chocolaty eyes, silky golden strands of her hair, her…."

Before he could say anything more he fell unconscious and Kimaya managed to lift him by her arms and dropped him at his seat. On the other hand, I was shedding huge tears of joy. He still loves me, I thought. I wandered that had brought a sudden change in him. I thought that he would never see my face again for the rest of his life. Kimaya needs to be taught a lesson and I will do the honors.

No matter how much we wrangle, Kimaya should not be a part of his life and I'm glad to hear that Rey is not yet captured by her charms like other men do when they ponder over an adorable woman. I was confident that the day is not too far away when he will separate from her forever. A few minutes later Robert sat next to me and ordered me to hide myself.

"If you are caught with me in this flight alive then you know you won't be alive later. Be cautious. I fail to understand that you have humiliated Rey to a greater extent, have slandered him in public, yet he is still in love with you. I must say that he is a dim-witted fellow. He does not have any self-respect."

"He is not dim-witted, you are. This is the brawn of love that is drawing him closer to me every moment."

"Don't start off again. Just beware."

"I hope so that you seem to have forgotten that Rey is not alone in this flight. Kimaya is accompanying him too."

"I forget to tell you that Kimaya is also in my hands. She too is involved in all this but as a villain. We are partners in this crime. She wanted to marry Rey and that could have been possible only if you are out of his life forever."

"As expected. I was aware of all this before."

"Preserve your anger for some other day. She too is a villain. I'm sure that you never expected that your best friend will turn out to be your foe."

He burst out a wicked laughter and left after warning me again. I was too terrified. He was correct for the first time. I never expected Kimaya to be a part of all this.

I had a quick glance at the back. Robert held Kimaya's hands and took her along somewhere out of anyone's notice. I decided to chase them. I hid myself behind a partition. They were standing beside the washroom door and were gossiping. I listened.

"Rob I forewarned you not to ever meet me again. Then what the hell are you doing here?"

"First tell me what the hell are you doing in this flight?"

"I asked you first, stop double crossing me you cheat. By the way, congratulations, she is dead."

"She is alive. I won't let her die soon, especially after all the miseries that her mother has caused me."

"Great."

"What is wrong with your Rey?"

"He is going out of control. We were living happily but till yesterday. He appeared disturbed to me yesterday and I'm not able to comprehend that why he reacted in this manner today."

"Tell me everything from the start."

She went on narrating the whole incident to him and I continued to hear their conversation which I found fruitful. All my hopes that were long dead, rose up attaining a new life of gloominess. I felt that Rey was aware of my presence. Now I can ensure my escape and also that these villains will suffer for all this soon.

"I don't think so that he is aware that she loves him too," continued Kimaya.

"Have a control over your husband. As it is I hate him and if he tries to cross my way then he'll die and if he'll ruin my plan then you'll die too. Do you understand you freaking….."

"Have a control over your tongue. It's running too often nowadays. Control it or before he discovers that she's alive."

"Right. So, hasta la vista."

"Goodbye."

I quietly rose up and sat on my seat and counterfeited to be asleep. He sat next to me and I could sense him staring me. Yet I did not open my eyelids because that is what he wanted me to do. After a few minutes of stare, he fell asleep and I, seeking the opportunity, was seeking for Rey but he was not seated on his seat. I noticed Kimaya searching for him too and so I went back to my place and slept too.

After five hours we landed at the airport and grabbing our luggage in our hands we slid outside and waited for a cab to drop us to our venue. Robert commanded me to wait till he gets a cab. After he left, a hand pulled me and I saw a man urging me to follow him. His face was covered by a muslin cloth. He pulled me hurriedly and took me to a corner inside the airport where only we two were present. He uncovered his face.

"Rey, what are you doing over here?"

"I love you Stella."

"I'm not Stella, I'm Rose and I don't know you so just get lost and let me go. Leave me alone."

I tried to free my arm but he held it tightly. He bent forward and kissed me and then he let me free. For a minute even I forgot everything and kissed him back. I later realized what I was doing and so I pulled him back.

"Please leave. I don't know you."

"Then why did you kiss me back."

"It's because you provoked me to do so. I'm Rose, and I don't think so Sir that I'm of any use to you."

"Stella I've read your diary, I know why you refused my proposal. Stella I need to know the rest of it from you. Who is that bastard who is torturing you, blackmailing you?

Don't lie this time. I'm waiting. Proceed since we don't have much time to waste."

"I love you Rey."

With tears rolling in my eyes I embraced him. My arms didn't let him off since it was the thirst that was longing for since five years.

Chapter 14

"Rey I'll update you with every trivial issue but you have to be dumb after that since it is the matter of survival. We must be careful and must deal with each and every thing with set ups."

"I understand and I promise you that I'll get you out of this trap as soon as possible and I'm sorry that you are suffering because of me. Trust me, we'll be together. I love you."

"I love you too, but he is too dangerous. He is extremely cunning. Don't feel sorry about anything. Your life is my life too and I'm just saving my life."

"No more of it now. Let's get out of here. Then we'll deal with him later."

"No I can't escape until I get the clues. If you want to help me out then please let me know if we can trap him too."

"First tell me that who is he and why is he seeking revenge."

"The man behind all this is Robert."

"What? He married you forcefully and treated you like a slave."

"Not only he but your wife Kimaya too is involved in this. Let me tell you everything from the beginning. He is Robert Patrick, Steve Patrick's son. Do you know who he was?"

"He is that womanizer and rapist's son. I've heard about him. He was a flirt who had many affairs in his whole lifetime- around 58 I think, or maybe more. Whosoever used to refuse to sleep with him was blackmailed. First he would change his disguise according to the woman's likings, offer them lots of drinks and would take their advantage and also record it to humiliate them further. No one ever had the audacity to report against him. He was one of the richest millionaires of his times."

"My mother was a journalist and one of her friends was a victim of his traps too. She informed mom of this and so mom decided to trap him either. She risked her life to save millions of lives. She went up to him and decided to shoot his crimes. She shot him while he was molesting a lady in his room. The next day he confessed his crimes automatically before her confessing that she is the first lady he has fallen in love with."

"How are you so sure that he was in love with her?"

"He gave her all the tapes that he had recorded in past and said that her love has transformed him completely and so he promised her to alter his habits for her sake."

"Oh my God! What did your mom do after that? Did she handed over the tapes to the police department or was she in love with him too?"

"She didn't reciprocate his love. She promised to marry him the next day. That night she did hand over the tapes to police and narrated them the whole incident. Next day she dressed up in a white gown to break his heart and to teach him what a heart break is. She telecasted the tape that she had shot and the cops arrested him."

"I must say that your mother did a great job. She was a very bold and courageous woman. Was he the one who killed her?"

"Nope. Rob is my mother's murderer."

"But I fail to understand that why is Rob after our lives?"

"After the brutal black mailings and all, Steve was hung to death and Rob was just seven when his father died. His mother committed a suicide when she discovered the real intentions of Steve. She was totally the opposite of her husband. Rob was self born. He only bore one maxim in his brain- REVENGE."

While narrating the incident I started sobbing and Rey consoled me with the sympathetic love and comforted me by making me feel his presence and convincing me that I'm not alone anymore.

"To seek revenge he first killed my mom. He wants to torment me and make my life hell because he wants me to be alone like he had been in his father's absence. One day while Serena visited my house, she saw Rob inside my house and heard him yelling at my picture and planning out the rest. He felt her presence, caught her and killed her too. He also killed James because he saw him at my house seeking for clue against him. You remember the message."

"Yes, I do."

"It was scrapped with James's blood. Poor couple, they died without any fault. He was aware of our love for each other and so he separated us too. He tried to contact Kimaya and informed her of our love and they both were involved in creating misunderstandings between us. I never expected my best friend to ditch me."

"That wicked lady, and I loved such a woman."

"You love her?"

"I tried to, but failed to delete you from my life. I was just trying to move on. I'm sorry."

"I understand."

"But Stella how was he so alert about each and every action of your life?"

"One night I was deeply hurt after breaking your heart and so I broke the mirror of my washroom and to my dismay I witnessed a secret room from which Robert used to secretly watch me out and all that we did. There were miniature cameras attached to all my clothes with microphone. He told me the entire story and warned me that if I removed these cameras even for a sec, he would hand over your video clips to cops. So I could not inform you about anything."

"What about your death?"

"It was pre-planned. I did as he instructed. After telecasting it live we shifted to Bangkok and there he made sure that I had no contact with anyone. He had an eye on me 24*7. The camera recently broke this morning and so I was waiting for the opportunity to inform you."

"Stella what are his intentions now? Tell me before anything goes wrong."

"He is planning to….."

Before I could discuss the robbery plan, I heard Robert yelling out my name and so I requested Rey to leave. He did so and left. I lied on the ground and pretended to swoon. Robert came lifted me up and took me away in a cab.

Chapter 15

Rey was still depressed over everything. He returned back and decided firmly to rescue me from Rob's trap. While he was walking Kimaya came rushing towards him, shouting out his name.

"Honey where were you? I was looking for you since so long. Don't leave me alone in this unfamiliar place. We are here to spend some time together."

Rey stared at her with those prickly looks and without a pause slapped her. A huge crowd surrounded them and all the eyes were fixed on them. His eyes were blood red with rage. Kimaya rose up in dismay.

"Are you mad? How dare you slap me publicly?"

"Shut up. Stop pretending to love me. I know what you are up to and you better stay away from me from now onwards before I give you another one. You've been cheating me for such a long time and I like a fool trusted you blindly. No more of it now. Get one thing straight into your head that I am not interested in you. We did land over here for a sweet romantic honeymoon but now I want a divorce from you, right now."

"Please don't say so. It's hurting me. It's pinching me every corner of my heart."

"Fake, everything is fake. Listen I'm sending you the divorce papers so sign them and get going and don't you ever try to contact me after that. My heart knows I much I loved Stella and I'll always do and I'll never forgive you for separating us."

"What? When did I do all this? In fact she was the one who did so. That bloody ….."

"Kimaya just shut up."

"Who told you all this?"

"I heard your whole conversation with Robert in flight. You are responsible for her death. I hate you."

Kimaya thought, "He thinks that she is still dead. I still have the chance to afflict him with my charms. Kimaya try twisting the tale. I can't afford to lose him."

"It is all true but let me explain once. I did support Rob in all this but what's the big deal about this. Everyone does that to win her lover's heart and even I did so. At least I showed her true colors to you. If she would have been sincere she would have married you and not him. I am the correct life partner for you."

"Do you even realize what you've done, because of you she ….just forget it."

"No, tell me, don't ignore this time. I want to know my fault. If you won't tell I won't leave you. She might have liked you a bit but I love you and this is not dangerous for her."

"If you have ever loved me then please leave me alone."

"I can't do that."

Rey kept on recounting the whole incident word by word and as he spoke Kimaya's eyes were filled with tears of guilt and rage.

"Rey please trust me, I was not aware of all this. Rob just told me that he loves her and he wants her like I do and we just had a deal. I never expected that he wanted to marry her for all this. I'm really sorry for her."

"Just stop it now. Your fake concern won't melt me this time. I'm leaving you right now."

Rey left immediately and Kimaya weept with guilt and fell on the ground banging the floor and yelling with agony. People came up to her and requested her to rest somewhere. She went to the hotel room where they were about to spend their vacation. Rey was missing.

Hours passed by and there was no sign of Rey. She called her but he disconnected her calls. She felt that it was pointless waiting for her since the offence she did was not worth forgiveness. She decided to rectify her mistakes and thought, "I'm sorry Stella and Rey. I know you won't forgive me ever. But at least give me a chance to undo everything. Today I take an oath that I'll get you back together and would save you from that scoundrel."

She knew what she had to do next. After an hour she went up to Rey who sat in a melancholic tone. She felt sorry for him and apologized. He did not accept her apology. He rather requested her to leave.

"Rey I'm not as I had been before. Here take these divorce papers. I've signed it. I did all that was possible to win your heart, but I lost you forever, even as a friend now. I can't change what destiny has already decided. Maybe I deserved it, but you don't deserve to stay alone for the rest of your life. Instead of wasting your time, go look for her. She needs you."

Rey was aware of the sudden change in her. He could notice that in her eyes. He stopped himself, thinking that it might be another trap for him. Without uttering a word, he left her and did not turn back even once. Somewhere deep within she wished him luck and left too. Now Rey's target was fixed. He must save the love of his life.

"Stella where the hell were you?"

"I was lying unconscious you moron."

"Remember, tomorrow is the day and if you fail to do so, bear the consequences yourself. In fact the whole world would be after you then."

"I know. I need some rest."

"Good night for now coz tomorrow you'll be over baby."

"We'll see that who'll die at the end."

Chapter 16

It was twelve at night. It was time to bring the plan into action. Robert instructed me to enter and get the stuff done as soon as possible. I was extremely anxious. I tried to convince my heart saying All for Rey. It's the only chance to save myself and my love. I can't afford to lose this time.

All the doors were shut. I tried to figure out a way to enter from the map. To my dismay, all the entrances were locked and were under tight security. There were two watchmen, guarding each entrance. Further, there were CCTV cameras all around the complex. I had only an hour to execute the entire robbery and it seemed that not only the entrance doors were shut, but also the doors of all hopes were shut. My heart was thumping with fear. I must find a way to enter.

Suddenly a thought struck in my mind. I took a piece of stone from the ground and broke a window. I immediately hid myself and watched. All the watchmen gathered around the area. I took advantage of this and entered from the main entrance door.

There was darkness all around. Everything was still and silent. I searched for my torch and found my way out through this immense darkness. I paused for a moment and had a look over the guide map once again. I didn't have much time to fritter away. I quickly had a glance and rolled it back. The statue was secure upstairs on the fifteenth floor. If I used the elevator, it would create a big racket and it'll indicate the watchmen that I'm in and they'll get hold of me. The only option left was to climb the stairs up to fifteenth floor which is time as well as stamina consuming. Without wasting much more time I rushed upstairs without a break, and when I finally touched the steps of the fifteenth floor. I was almost panting and my clothes were soaked with sweat. I rested for a minute or so, and then had a look over the map again. According to it, I had to cross the world class security to reach the statue.

I took out the glasses from my bag. These were not simple glasses but special viewing glasses through which I could have a clear vision of the invisible beams of red light that acted like an alarm if touched. I need to go across this. There were many zig-zag, criss-cross, and other unusual patterns of light up to the rim to be crossed. It was almost impossible to do so. I thought of something else. I went up to the steel pole, which was the controller of the red laser. I must hack this fast.

I took off the code breaking device and set on to work. It was my first trial to hack a security device. It was a great risk indeed. I have mastered this hacking course when I was seventeen. I never attempted to hack anything yet. After a few minutes of coding, encoding and decoding, I lifted my arms to murmur a few words of prayer and pressed the

ENTER KEY. To my dismay, I was successful in breaking the security code and the laser beam vanished, making the way clear for me to enter.

I came forth the next security- the sensors, if they detected any human footprint, or sensed any human scent they would signal the guards immediately, second form of an alarm. I went inside the control room and was successful in breaking this code too. Then I went on and on till I broke the second last security code. I stood before the statue which was glittering in delight, reflecting its worth. It was secure surrounded by a glass covering, guarded by a machine which would only open if the password is entered. It could not be hacked. I had only five attempts.

I decided to first enter the owner's name. I typed GEORGE SUZERRIA. It declined. Then I typed the statue's title, LOVING SOUL, it declined again. Three more attempts left. Next I typed his wife's name JESSICA. It declined. My heart was beating heavily. I then wandered about the theme of the sculpture and typed LOVE. It declined. My last attempt and if I failed, the alarm would ring and all my efforts would go in vain. I took a deep breath and thought. Then I wandered that love without sacrifice is inappropriate. With a deep sigh I typed, LOVE AND SACRIFICE. I was flabbergasted when it showed on the screen ACCEPTED.

The glass case opened and the sculptor was burnishing its luster. I attempted to lift it but all in vain. How to carry this downstairs? I gave a call to Rob and instructed him to gather outside the window pane so that I can pass on the sculptor to him and get rid of all this as soon as possible. He texted me when he reached and I peeked down the window.

He waved me. I immediately tied the rope around it and made sure that it did not loosen up later. I then dragged it and dropped it down the window and slowly I loosened the rope to let it fall freely but without getting damaged. He caught hold of it and went away after a few minutes.

Now it was time for me to escape and I patted myself for conducting such a peril robbery ever and all alone. I smirked at the thought of getting rid of this slavery. I was about to leave when I heard the sound of footsteps climbing upstairs, I was terrified. I held the rope and tied it immediately to a pole and climbed downstairs hurriedly. They leaned down the window. Creep, they saw me escaping but failed to see my face as it was hidden under a cap.

As soon as my feet touched the ground I ran as fast as my feet could take me away. I was figuring out the way to escape but was trapped. Within a few seconds a huge police force surrounded every corner of the building and it was impossible for me to escape now. I decided to hide myself and immediately hid myself behind a banister.

I could not see but their voices could be heard clearly. They were making an announcement about the stolen sculptor. I stayed still and after an hour I peeked. They had already left. I stood up and was leaving when a hand caught hold of mine and I was handcuffed.

It was one of the cops. They were hidden too to catch hold of me. Dammmm. I was dead now.

He smiled and said, "Lady you are under arrest."

Chapter 17

Rey woke up early the next day and after consuming his refreshments he held the newspaper in his hands and read. He was astonished as he read the breaking news. He dropped the newspaper on the floor and immediately switched on the television and put the news channel.

The news channel highlighted the breaking news of the day – The most terrific robbery ever taken place. The world famous and the costliest sculptor ever of Flip Flop Lady, has been stolen.

The reporter said, "The Flip Flop Lady platinum sculptor has been stolen from the largest shopping complex in Paris. The culprit managed to break through all the security and fool the guards. The culprit has been arrested but the sculptor is still missing. According to the policemen she did not step out of the building after conducting the robbery. Then the question arises that where has the sculptor gone then? The person behind all this is a lady."

The news channel highlighted my picture and Rey was stunned. The reporter continued, "She is the same. Her name is Rose Patrick. Look at her ladies and gentlemen. Can you believe it that she can steal this? But she did. She is an international criminal now. It's only her footprints that have entered inside after 12:30."

"What the fuck is this? She is innocent. Was this the thing she wanted to discuss with me about? I need to prove her innocence before she is sentenced to lifetime imprisonment. I'm sure Robert might have blackmailed her again. Alas! Poor, naive lady."

When he turned back he slammed with Kimaya. He muttered a few abuses and rose up. Kimaya stopped him.

He shouted, "Are you mad? Listen I don't have time for all your crab so let me leave. I have to save her. She needs me."

"I heard everything and was aware of it before you."

"Just let me go."

With guilt in her eyes she pulled out the divorce papers from the back and handed it over to him.

"Here, I've signed it. I'm really guilty and please give me a last chance to mend everything."

"I accept your apology but please leave right now."

"I can help you in this. I know where he is. Just do as I say."

"You do, that's great. Thank you. Let's leave immediately then and get that bastard."

"Get inside the cab. I'll explain you on the way."

Once they were seated inside she drove the cab hurriedly and continued with her conversation, confessing all that she did in past and apologizing for every bit.

"Wait, let me call him. I'll act as if I'm still the female villain. Don't speak a word and let me make him confess everything. We'll record this while I'll be in a conversation with him."

"But Kimaya, you'll be arrested after that as you'll be confessing your intentions too and I don't want that."

"Rey, I've done something evil and I have to face the consequences. He's a killer and indeed a very witty one. Only I can trap him. So don't disturb me and let me call him. Here the ring is going. Keep shut now."

"Hello Kimaya babes."

"I heard the news. Congratulations bro, you did it finally. So you are the man who did all this?"

"Yes I am the same. I am the one who blackmailed her to steal and I am the one who treated her like a slave these past few years. I'm a devil and I accept it. I finally seek my revenge."

"I know. I have a great news for you. I have decided to marry you."

"Really. I love you baby."

"After all you are a rich man now and what to do with this Rey. He's so bugging. I want to be with you."

"Yes baby, I'll shower you with wealth if you'll do so."

"Since we are a couple now you need to tell me the truth of your life."

"Sure. So listen."

He began confessing each and every bit unaware of the fact that it's been recorded and Kimaya giggled as he continued to speak. She is an outstanding actor. She trapped the biggest criminal with her charms.

"So see you soon then."

"But I want to meet you now."

"Not now, I don't want you to be in danger."

"I'll book two flight tickets and we'll leave tomorrow morning itself."

"Definitely, but Rey what are you planning for today?"

"There are certain things left undone. Need to get done with that and satisfy my father's dead soul."

"What is it?"

"Tell you tomorrow. It's the end of all."

After saying so the connection was dead and Kimaya panicked. Both of them wandered what is he up to now?

"Rey I'm driving fast. Everything has been recorded. Take the earphones and listen to it once. I'm rushing to the police station as we need to get Stella out of there as soon as possible."

"Yup."

On their way they were caught in a traffic jam. Kimaya cursed and yelled out, "What the fuck? How to reach the station now before it is too late?"

"Don't worry about it. I'll drop you there soon and you'll be together again?"

"Kimaya relax, thank you so much."

"It's my pleasure Rey."

"I have edited the recording and I've removed your part from it. You have realized your fault and so I don't want you to be behind the bars."

"But Rey..."

"No ifs and buts now. You are a great friend. My decision is final and don't you dare try to alter it."

"Thanks, and it's really sweet of you. Do you think Stella will forgive me too?"

"She would, positively, after all there is no difference between her and me. We are two bodies yet one soul."

"Hope that you both are united again."

"It's just a matter of few hours now. Today itself I'll marry her and I give you the first invitation."

"Sure Mr. Romeo."

Chapter 18

"I said I was the one who stole it so why are you tormenting me further. I have confessed my crime. All the proofs are against me. You have several eye witnesses. Still you don't believe me?"

"Nobody is convinced that such a sweet and innocent looking lady can actually raid to such a great extent. I know you are not alone in this, there has to be someone else too involved in it. So tell me, who's your crime partner?"

"No one. It will be my final answer no matter whether you ask it once, twice or thousand times."

"Lady till now I was polite to you. Now you'll see the harsher side of mine. Mala."

A lady superintendant entered and he whispered something in her ears. She nodded her head and approached me fulfilling the orders given to her. She locked the gate and started hammering me. I yelled and yelled and cried with agony. I bore the pain and my entire body had the red marks of canning. She didn't pause. Even I didn't confess anything coz I knew that the tapes are still with Rob. When she got pissed off she left me alone weeping.

I must get out of here before it's too late. I'm still not secure, not even Rey. Once I get hold of those tapes and photographs and destroy them, then I'll make all the confessions. Till then I must keep mute.

After an hour Rey and Kimaya entered the station and called out for the commissioner. He came up to him and Rey pleaded him to leave me. He refused to do so.

"Sir please, she is innocent."

"You call this lady innocent? You must be joking."

"Sir she did so under pressure. I have witnesses and all the evidences against the real culprit."

He went on and on narrating him the entire plot, skipping his and Kimaya's role in between. The officer listened with pity for me and feelings of agony for Robert.

"But how do you know so much about her?"

"Coz I love her. I've always loved her. Sir she has suffered misery and treachery these past years. She needs tender love now that only I can give her. Please, I beg of you sir."

"Then why didn't you inform this before? Maybe we could have saved her earlier only."

Rey hesitated to answer. Kimaya held his hand and replied, "Sir, a few years back, the media telecasted that Stella Stewart is dead and so we thought that she might be dead. But when we heard the news today morning we immediately came up to you. That's all."

"Where did you get these evidences from?"

Rey burst out in agony and roared, "Just get her out of that bloody hell before I thrash you. Get her out right now. Is this the time to inquire about such senseless issues? I want to meet her so will you just hurry. After that, carry on with the investigation. I'm dying to meet her."

"But she has already left half an hour back."

"How? When? With whom?"

"Rey calm down, sir please don't mind. He's just worried."

"I understand. A man came up to me before you and gave me this video in which she has already been proved innocent."

He played the entire video. Surprisingly, the video was edited and my face was replaced with somebody else's.

"The man told me that she was just passing by when she saw the culprit escaping and was just trying to chase her. Unfortunately, the real culprit escaped and she was arrested indeed."

"Who was the man who handed over this video?"

"Charles Patrick."

Rey suspected the man to be Robert when he heard 'Patrick'. He searched for Robert's picture in his wallet and grabbing it he inquired whether he is the same.

"Yes, he is the one."

"Are you silly, he is Robert? He is a murderer. Stella is in danger. Let's go before he does anything to her."

"Gentlemen we will accompany you both and get hold of that criminal."

"Please don't, you've already ruined everything."

"We are not asking, we are ordering, it's our duty."

"If you'll accompany us he'll kill her."

"Keep your cell phones on. We'll trace your location and reach there when you'll text us. Beware and take care."

"Kimaya you stay and let me go."

"No I will accompany you."

"Come then, let's hurry."

Chapter 19

"Where the hell are you taking me Robert? Till now I did as you told me to and you clearly said that if I'll hand over the statue to you, then you'll spare my life forever."

"I said that if you'll be back safe Miss Stewart. But you were behind the bars and I don't give my right of humiliating you, to anyone else in this world."

The car stopped before a huge villa and he dragged me inside. His pull was hurting me but I didn't utter a word. He dropped me on the floor with a thud and I bellowed. He then brought the tapes, pictures and a revolver, which seemed fully loaded. He showed me the photographs one by one.

"Here Stella, these are the evidences you've been after for such a long time. Take them and get lost."

I was about to snatch them from his hands when he pulled it back and pushed me back. He pointed his revolver in my direction and smirked.

"Do you really think that I'll make this so undemanding? Let's play the last game of life. If you win, these will be all yours along with your life and if you lose then you'll lose your life as well as your Rey forever."

"I don't trust you this time so just hand over these videos to me."

"My darling Stella, not so soon. I'll be hiding these somewhere inside this villa and you must find them and destroy them yourself and you just have five minutes to do so."

"Just stop playing games with me and do as I say. I've had enough of you. Now you can't provoke me to follow your instructions blindly."

"I love this flame in your eyes. Just do as I say."

He made me sit on a chair and tied my hands to it. He then fled away and hid the evidences and within a few minutes arrived at the spot. He indicated me that my time had started at that moment. I yelled at him to untie me but he refused.

I somehow struggled and undid the rope and was free to move. I went to his bedroom and searched for it. No sign of it at all. I had a glance over the clock hung at the wall. I had only two more minutes to accomplish it. Then I assumed that he must have hid that behind the mirror. I immediately went to the washroom and opened the mirror door. Yes, I did it. I grabbed them and tore the pictures into tiny thousands of bits. I took a rod and destroyed the tapes too. Then I breathed out a deep sigh of relief and freedom. I don't trust Rob. Before he gets too know that I've got hold of it, I need to leave.

Rey ordered Kimaya to pace up the vehicle. He was breathless at that moment praying for my safety.

"Kimaya are you sure that both of them will be there only?"

"Yes I'm completely positive about it. It is the same place that he had texted me this morning. He wanted me to meet him tomorrow at the same venue. So he ought to be there."

"I hope she's alright. Please save her Jesus."

"Don't worry, she's a brave girl and she'll handle it."

"I know that but I don't trust that wicked Robert. Please hasten. I want her back safe and secure. I won't be able to forgive myself if anything goes wrong with her and I won't be able to love anyone else except the one who actually devoted her entire life to my love."

"Please calm down. We'll be there soon."

"Hopefully."

"Just be positive and hope for the best."

Robert suddenly shot me at the back and I groaned with agony. It was hurting like a devil. Blood was oozing out flowing immensely. I fell on the floor and smirked at him. He came forward and placed his revolver touching my forehead.

"I won't let you live peacefully Miss Stewart, you must die."

"I've destroyed everything and now even if you'll shoot me I won't refuse because I've given my life to Rey already. You are over. Do what you feel like now and I promise I won't yell. My body might die but my loving soul will be alive and even you can't kill it."

"But there is nobody to care for you and love you Stella. The entire world is after your life. People loathe you, especially your so called love, Rey."

"That's your misconception Rob. You are already finished. I met Rey at the airport and enlightened him with everything. So if you still think that you can escape, you are highly mistaken. He'll take your life if you'll take mine."

He smacked my face and pulled my hair and I struggled hard so that he could release me. The bullet was yet inside my flesh and it was burning my soul and I flushed out my tears with anger and pain. He roared louder and louder.

After a few minutes Rey and Kimaya entered the villa and Rey was astonished when he found me lying dead and shot. He pampered and moaned near my carcass. He held my head by his arms and continued to moan. Kimaya too accompanied him in his moan.

Kimaya decided to end Robert's life too and Rey swore to kill him. Kimaya sympathized with Rey and requested him to stay calm till they get hold of him.

Kimaya called Robert and he told her everything and pleaded her to meet him at the back of this villa, where he was secretly hidden.

"I've got the bookings done. We ought to leave right now. Do one thing don't meet me here, reach the airport as soon as possible. We'll depart after an hour and start with our new life. I'll wait for you there."

He disconnected the call and Robert was about to leave when Kimaya came there and he stopped.

"Kimaya what are you doing over here?"

"I was worried."

"Let's leave this place before we are caught."

"There is no need for you to take so much of pains. I've planned out something else and probably a better option for you."

"What?"

She immediately pulled out a revolver and shot him thrice and he fell dead on the floor. Rey entered and hugged her. They dragged his corpse next to Stella's corpse and Rey placed Kimaya's revolver on the ground. After a few minutes cops entered and a huge investigation was carried out.

"I lost my love forever."

"We are really sorry to hear about such a big loss of yours Mr. Rey. I hope you won't mind me asking you something. Who shot Robert?"

Rey saw Kimaya who was panicking with fear and guilt. Rey replied, "Stella shot him back when he shot him. Now please can you leave me alone and let me moan in peace."

"Thank you for your co-operation, please you both may leave now."

Kimaya took him outside and questioned him for hiding the reality to which he replied, "I don't punish guilty people and you did that for Stella and I'm sure she too would have never wanted you to be arrested for killing the man who made her life hell on earth. May her soul rest in peace."

"Forgive me Stella for all that I did in past. Rest in peace."

Chapter 20

Kimaya was eagerly waiting for Rey inside the church. She was dressed for a marriage. Yes, she will marry Rey the same day. Rey has already moved on. After fifteen minutes Rey entered and so did the father. Rey gave a soft kiss on her cheeks and whispered, "Looking gorgeous."

Father proceeded with the wedding ceremony, "Do you Miss Kimaya, accept Rey as your lawfully wedded husband?"

"I do."

"And do you Mr. Rey accept Kimaya as your lawfully wedded wife?"

There was a complete silence for a while and Rey appeared disturbed. He hesitatingly answered, "I do."

"Congratulations to both of you. You're married now."

There was an atmosphere of gloominess that day. People celebrated the moment and Kimaya was glad too. But Rey still seemed disturbed and guilty. Kimaya held his hand and they both left after an hour. They reached their home and Kimaya served wine in two glasses. She offered one glass to Rey but he refused. She insisted him to have a sip and he took the glass from her hand.

"My life seems incomplete by her absence. She made a big difference and I can never forget the lady who died for my sake. She gave me a new life and bought colors in my fade life. I love her and I hope you understand that. And……."

He paused and cackled aloud with a big smile and so did Kimaya. He wrapped his arms around her and pulled her towards himself.

"I'm so done with this pretence of loving her. The truth is that I've always loved one lady and that's you."

She patted his back and replied, "Thank God, I thought that you have changed. Poor she, I really pity her. She actually died for her so called love, who is actually the villain of this story."

"Very true and how could I love her? She died in that big misconception. It was all pre-planned. I'll be thankful since she saved my life."

"What if she would have been alive? For a minute this thought made me grief-stricken and I can't even express how glad I was when I found her dead."

"I would have shot her if she would have been alive, after all why to bear excess baggage with ourselves."

"You're right."

"She was actually the dumbest woman ever born on earth. That Robert bastard used to blackmail me too. When I got to know about his revenge, I had a deal with him that I can help him seek revenge with her but in return he must return the fake video tapes."

He continued to narrate his evil plans. "I convinced him that I'll create such circumstances that she would hand over herself to him. I intentionally took admission in the same college and made her feel attracted towards me."

"How did you get to know that I love you?"

"I heard yours and Stella's conversation, honestly speaking I was attracted towards you too but I was afraid of reciprocating love when I knew that you were her close friend. You might warn her."

"Then when did you start trusting me?"

"When I was convinced that you can do anything for me and so I involved you too in this plan. I sent you to Rob so that he does not doubt us. I made her love me to that extent that she can sacrifice anything for my love's sake."

"And she actually did. You are seriously a magician."

"Thank you sweetheart. Then I pretended as if I love her too. The most irritating job I ever did. She was so irritating."

"I see, but why did you pretend that you loathe me and told me to do the same as if we are actually unaware of everything."

"You remember the wedding night."

"Yes."

"I was about to make love to you when I noticed a camera keeping an eye on us and I was sure that it was all Rob's efforts to keep an eye on us and so I had to be harsh to you so that everything seems natural."

"Alright."

"Why did you shoot him when our way was already clear?"

"He might create a trouble for us later and so I found it convenient to kill him rather than taking a risk again because fools like Stella are not always there to save our lives."

"Smart woman, I must say. Finally we are living our lives happily now."

"Yup. But why did you slap me publicly, that was rude?"

"I've already apologized to you for that, but I had to do this. I can't take the risk. He might have watched us. Now no evidences against me and I'm free from that title of a 'CRIMINAL'."

"I missed you so much."

"Missed you too baby."

"I love you."

"I love you too."

Printed in the United States
By Bookmasters